THE VERDICT

THE VERDICT

T. L. SANDS

Text copyright © Tonie Louise Sands.

The moral rights of the author have been asserted.

First published in 2025 by Kingston University Press

All rights reserved. No part of this publication may be reproduced or transmitted, in any form or by any means electronic or mechanical, including photocopy, recording, or any information storage and retrieval system, without prior permission of the publisher.

Every effort has been made to fulfil requirements with regard to reproducing copyright material. The publisher will be glad to rectify any omissions at the earliest opportunity.

These stories are works of fiction. Any resemblance to real person living or dead is purely coincidental.

A catalogue of this book is available from the British Library.

ISBN 978 1 909362 89 5
Typeset in Bebas Neue, Montserrat and Times New Roman

Cover illustration by Sophie Burchell.
Editorial and Design by Kingston MA Publishing Students: Sophie Burchell, Raphaela Craveiro, Miya Libman, Alessandra Rizzi, and Nicholas Pinto.

KINGSTON UNIVERSITY PRESS
Kingston University
Penrhyn Road
Kingston-Upon-Thames
KT1 2EE

For Abbe Fletcher, Nelson Douglas,

and in remembrance of Mick Kennedy,

whose influence remains.

THE VAULT

THE VAULT

THE VAULT

Alison flinched awake, the SoulLink Node in her neck whirring to life, steady and relentless as it listened in. Slowly, she slipped out of bed, muscles tight, mind alert, careful not to wake the beast recording her every move. She watched the hulking mass of a man as his chest rose and fell in an unfeeling rhythm that sucked the life from the room. Moving like a ghost, she glided toward the bathroom, pulling the door shut gently, as though the latch might betray her. In the dim light, she sank onto the toilet, head lulling into her hands. The air thick and suffocating, as she gulped for breath, trying to keep herself from unravelling. She watched as her heart rate decreased to a slow pump on her Fitbit to her meditative state, the chip in her neck slipped back into sleeping mode and powered itself down. He could hear her every move now and she wasn't in the habit of talking to herself. Tonight, her mind felt wild, untamed. A flash of longing bloomed hot and angry – an image of herself and Stevie, her little hand curled into hers, running far from here, from him.

It had taken three years of hell to summon the courage to leave him and the journey had been arduous and slow. For the most part, Alison had spent much of it in a slumber so deep it was as if she had slipped into a coma. At times, she felt as though she had died, as if she were watching her life like a shoddy rerun of some forgotten daytime TV drama. She had wondered what it would take, how much more she could endure before she could break free of her own Groundhog Day, free from the feeling of eyes always watching. *Keep it together*, she whispered to herself as her pulse began to rise. Tom's heavy breathing lingered through the walls. She pressed her palms against her eyes, as if to squeeze the thoughts back in, to push them down before the implant registered them. She could feel the SoulLink powering back up, readying itself to read her, rifling through the corners of her mind. She had no place to run, no place to hide. Tom had made sure of that. Stevie's face flickered in her mind, eyes wide and waiting in the driveway for her, the repeated resolve settling over her, heavy but sharp. *Stop it!* she told herself, feeling the familiar burn of the thought.

One day, they would run, and she'd tear this thing out of her neck. She would rip herself free of him, blood and all, if it meant keeping Stevie safe. She gulped and swallowed down what felt like a ball of lead. She would pay for that in the morning. It would be the first thing he saw, and he would be angry.

▶❙❙

She was right. That morning, she saw her own blood blossom into Stevie's orange juice, swirling bright red like grenadine. Beneath the table, Stevie clung to her leg screaming. Tom never hit her in the face if he could help it, but today he had been so very angry. Alison had tried to hold her breath, stifling the cries so Stevie wouldn't notice, but it was no use. Blood spilled from her nose like a broken faucet. Another strike, and she was flat on her back now, sliding to a halt. He stepped over her, giving her one sharp kick to the ribs before slamming the door behind him.

Alison lay there, breath kicked clean out of her, dazed and gasping at the air, relieved it had been over quickly. Stevie peered out from beneath the tablecloth, eyes wide. Alison lay still, chest heaving for a second more, then stretched out her arm. Stevie scrambled to the freezer like they'd rehearsed, day after day, her tiny hands grabbing the frozen peas, clutching them to her chest, darting to the oven, tugging the tea towel free. Then she was ready, holding it out just so, her little hands practiced. Alison wrapped the peas, pressing them gingerly to her swelling face. A few tumbled free and scattered, rolling across the linoleum, and Stevie let out a delighted squeal.

'Peeeeas!' she shouted, clapping her hands. Alison gazed at her child, feeling a fury of molten lava bubbling up inside her.

For the past six months, resentment had taken root, spreading through her like rot. She had struggled to be as present for Stevie as she once was. She was in survival mode, her mind whirring in the background, plotting all the possible ways she could escape. Stevie seemed to sense the shift in her mother, her wide eyes flickering from Alison's clenched fists to her face, searching for reassurance. Alison felt the guilt seep in, cold and hard, like a weighted blanket. She opened her arms and Stevie crawled close, burying her face into her mother's chest, her little heart fluttering like a trapped bird. Alison tried to breathe through the pain, wondering what had possessed her to think about running, taking Stevie. He'd known she wanted to go back to work now that Stevie was in nursery, and she'd been so careful to stay in his good graces, hoping it would make him more agreeable when the time came. She had become what her mother used to call a well-trained dog. Always trying to be a good girl.

Fetch what he needed.

Keep quiet.

Be obedient.

She'd spent the last three years hoping she would be rewarded. A kind word, a little time alone. On the rare occasion when he did throw her a bone, he had always wanted something in return. She could count these occasions on one hand, and no matter how hard she tried, no matter how obedient she was, his treatment was vile, and the rules kept changing. As she lay there holding the peas to her face her mother's voice surfaced in her mind.

'What the hell are you still doing here Alison? Get up! Get out of here!'

'I can't. He'll kill me,' she squeezed her eyes shut.

'Exactly,' her mother's voice said, flat and sharp. 'One day, Ally. He'll fucking kill you.'

▶❚❚

Alison's heart thudded as she took Stevie into nursery the following week. Stevie bounded off without so much as a goodbye. Alison took a moment to settle her breathing, gripping the steering wheel with white-knuckled intensity. She couldn't afford to be careless. A few days prior, Alison had received an email that made her almost cry with relief. She was being assigned a new therapist, a woman. This one wasn't a friend of Tom's, wasn't someone who had already been primed to monitor her and report back. She had messaged the new therapist immediately, choosing her words carefully.

My husband arranged for my previous therapist through a personal connection, but I've never been able to speak openly. I have a SoulLink Node that my husband insisted on. At first it was to bring us closer together to share memories and connections. Eventually I found out he was using it to surveil and control me. It allows him to monitor my thoughts, emotions, even my memories. It powers down when I meditate, but he can still hear everything. Please do not reply to this email. He checks my mail. Just know that I'll be at the first appointment.

She signed off, deleted the message, and closed the laptop, praying that her small act of rebellion wouldn't be discovered.

At first, Tom had been so enthusiastic and supportive, framing the SoulLink as a way for them to share their most intimate thoughts. She'd hesitated, but Tom had been so understanding, so persuasive. Ultimately, she had accepted, thinking it might strengthen their relationship. For a while it had. She thought back to the nights when they first had the Node installed, where they shared their hopes and dreams. The control crept in like a slow poison, turning small arguments into red flags and reruns of the same conversations that would be played over. When she hesitated to answer him, he would grow angry and suspicious, then apologise. But as time went on there were more questions and no apologies, just Alison trying to defuse his temper and figure out what set him off.

The problems really started after Stevie was conceived. She'd had a fleeting, quiet regret about falling pregnant, a moment's reflection about the life she was leaving behind. Tom had found out and had turned her doubt into an accusation, insisting she wished their unborn child harm, had wished her dead, putting words in her mouth, twisting every thought. She had found out that he had been watching her for months, recording and archiving private moments of her mind. She threatened to leave, but when her mother died, Tom was all she had left. She owed it to Stevie to make a go of things.

Tom comforted her while using her grief as a weapon, prying into her thoughts and exploiting every crack he found. Whenever she sought a moment's peace to reflect or cry, he would accuse her of 'shutting him out.' He monitored her sadness through the Node, insisting he had the right to know how she was feeling for the safety of their unborn child. He didn't want her to 'end up like her mother,' who had lost her mind and Alison who had been taken into foster care. He didn't hit her then, but the abuse was suffocating.

Slowly, she'd distanced herself from her friends and family, dreading the explanations she'd have to give Tom afterwards about every word she'd said. By the time her employer reached out, asking if she planned to return to work, Tom had already laid the groundwork for her dismissal. If she dared try to return, he'd email her memories to the office: her unfiltered fantasies about a colleague, her moment of exasperation calling her boss an absolute imbecile and, worst of all, the unguarded confession she'd made to Tom in passing, criticising her best friend Jen as *utterly* useless and speculating that she'd only earned her director's position by sleeping with their older, married boss. The thoughts, meant to pass through her mind and vanish, now hung like a noose around her neck, keeping her bound to him. Memory by memory, her shame had stacked up to an insurmountable rockface that she couldn't climb.

The first slap had come during an argument about money. She'd asked if she could get a part time job after Stevie was born, thinking they could use the extra income. He'd exploded, calling her ungrateful and selfish. She stood her ground, refusing to back down. His hand lashed out. The shock of it left her stunned, but he had apologised immediately, crying and promising it wouldn't happen again.

But it did.

Each act of violence came with a justification that left her questioning whether she had done something to provoke him. When Alison tried to confide in the therapist Tom sought out for her, she was met with veiled indifference, their loyalty clearly with him. It became obvious that the entire arrangement was designed to gaslight her; to make her believe she was the problem. She left those sessions feeling more trapped than before.

▶II

Her new therapist had a quiet, softly lit office in an unassuming building, and Alison instantly felt the contrast between here and her prior therapist's office. Dr Anwar greeted her with a warm smile and a calm presence. She gestured to the couch and Alison sat, instinctively curling her hands in her lap. Dr Anwar sat opposite, giving her a moment to breathe.

'I'm glad you're here, Alison,' she said softly, letting the quiet fill the room.

Alison gave a small, nervous nod, her fingers tracing the seam of her jeans over her knees, feeling her heart race. She became aware of the implant in her neck, of Tom potentially listening in, catching every word.

'Before we begin, let's take a moment to breathe. Just you and me here,' Dr Anwar watched her carefully, her voice gentle but firm.

Following her lead, Alison inhaled deeply, holding the breath as instructed, then letting it out slowly. She focused on each breath, allowing it to soften her heartbeat, quiet her mind. Dr Anwar's voice wove through the silence, guiding her through deeper breathing, each inhalation and exhalation soothing the knot in her chest, the grip of fear loosening. Her pulse beginning to steady. Her mind drifted until the SoulLink Node powered down. Dr Anwar's voice was soft, a whisper now.

'Is there something you'd like to tell me, Alison?'

'I can't. . . I can't say much,' she said, her voice low, barely audible.

Dr Anwar raised a gentle hand, stopping her. Without a word she slid a small note across the table. Alison hesitated, then picked it up. The words, handwritten in neat, block letters, read: *He can only listen.* Alison felt a surge of power pulse through her, small but real, like the hint of a breeze on a stifling hot day.

'We don't have to rush,' she continued. 'Breathe deep and take it slow. Just tell me what you can. Even a little is a start.'

Alison stared at the notepad the doctor had placed before her, her hands trembling as bitterness surged within. She picked up the pen, searching for the words, and began to write, thoughts flooding out in careful, deliberate strokes.

He's in my head. Watching every move. Listening to every thought. I can't think freely. I've trained myself to live in this constant meditative state, where I dream of running, of finding a place where my thoughts are my own. Her words came out in a slow, careful stream onto the page, each one exposing itself, each one a small rebellion. *The SoulLink Node. It records everything. He has complete access. It only powers down when it thinks*

I'm asleep, but he can still hear if he's listening.

She took a breath, letting the small victory of sharing sink in. Dr Anwar nodded as if to say *I understand.* She picked up her own pen and scribbled something quickly before pushing the note across the table. *We'll talk, but we'll frame it around your mother. It's safer.* She tapped her fingers gently on the notepad while speaking aloud, the ruse of grief giving them cover while the real truths poured out onto paper.

At the end of the session, she set down her pen and gave Alison a task.

'For next time, I want you to try reaching out to one friend. Just one. It doesn't matter what happens. Even if it's just to apologise for your absence and let it sit there, that's enough.' Alison hesitated but agreed.

Jen had been her closest friend before Tom had systematically erased her connections. Alison lingered for a moment, her fingers brushing over her phone. The possibility of silence hung in the air. Even a single step forward was progress. As she left Dr Anwar's office, Alison felt a flicker of something she hadn't dared let herself feel. Hope. Sitting in her car, the weight of the session still pressing on her, she pulled her phone from her pocket. Her thumb hovered over the screen for a moment before she tapped out a message to Jen. It was simple, but it was a start:

Hi Jen. I know it's been a long time. I just wanted to say sorry for disappearing. I miss you. Let me know if you'd like to catch up sometime.

She hit send, her breath catching as the message disappeared into the void. For the first time since her mother had passed, she felt the faintest hint of a route forward. It wasn't much, but it was a beginning.

▶II

That evening Alison drove to pick Stevie up from school, where the fleeting pulse of hope was quickly swallowed by dread. She was barely through the door when Mrs Green approached her, her face a look of gentle concern. Alison's stomach twisted.

'Alison,' Mrs Green said quietly, drawing her aside. 'I wanted to have a quick word. Stevie's been saying some… troubling things about her father.'

A hot flush of shame prickled up Alison's neck. She could feel the bruises shining through the carefully applied concealer, ready to reveal her ruse. Alison could barely meet Mrs Green's eye, the horror of exposure flooding her, followed swiftly by a pulse of fear. Tom will see this, she thought. He'll know everything. She managed a weak smile, but her voice came out shrill.

'Oh, Stevie's got a vivid imagination. Kids, you know?'

'Of course,' Mrs Green replied. 'But… if there's anything you ever need to talk about, anything at all, please know we're here to help. We're always here.'

Mrs Green's eyes softened, her expression filled with an uncomfortable sympathy that made Alison shrink. She could feel Mrs Green's gaze drifting, reading every sign of strain etched on her face, stopping at the faint bump on the bridge of her nose that the concealer hadn't quite masked. Alison's throat tightened, her chest feeling like it was bound in iron. She gave a quick nod and managed a thank you then hurried out, clutching Stevie's hand so tightly her daughter whimpered in protest.

Alison loosened her grip as they reached the car, her hands still trembling. She could feel the stares of passersby as if every layer of her carefully crafted disguise had turned to wet tissue paper. A tear slipped down her cheek, burning hot against the cold of the afternoon. She wiped it away roughly and buckled Stevie into her seat. Sitting in the car, she took a deep breath, trying to compose herself and swallow down the panic rising in her chest. *What will I tell Tom?* The question lingered, a dark cloud of dread. She knew that somehow, he'd twist this, turn Stevie's words into an accusation against her, a new way to blame her for *dragging strangers into their private lives*. The SoulLink Node would have picked up everything. She could practically hear his voice already, chiding her for being so careless. He'd call her selfish, accuse her of poisoning Stevie's mind, of lying. Alison sat there, gripping the steering wheel, the weight Mrs. Green's words pressing down on her. She forced herself to breathe. *If I could just think straight, I could survive this.* But it felt impossible. Stevie's little voice broke through her thoughts, bringing her back to the moment.

'Mummy, are you okay?'

'Mummy's just a bit tired, sweetheart,' she replied, glancing at her daughter in the rear-view mirror.

She forced a smile, reaching back to give Stevie's hand a reassuring squeeze. She turned back to the road, the knot in her stomach tightening as she tried to anchor herself, to keep from spiralling. She could feel the weight of Tom's anger already, the hand around her throat. As she turned onto their road, her heart began to race, each beat hammering at her chest. What would she say to him? How could she make him believe it wasn't her fault, that she hadn't invited Mrs Green's questions? The thoughts spun in her mind, a desperate search for a way to soften the impact, to avoid another explosion. As she pulled into the driveway, she tried to push down the terror, bury it beneath the thinly cracked surface of calm that she presented to him. *Maybe he wasn't watching,* she told herself. *Maybe he hadn't seen it.* But as she placed the key in the lock and opened the front door, Tom was there waiting, his expression stark, a look that reached down into her core and twisted her inside out.

Forcing herself to stay steady, she knelt to help Stevie out of her shoes and coat.

'Go play in the living room, sweetheart,' she said cheerfully.

She shut the door and stepped into the hallway, wondering if she would walk away from this.

'Do you know what you've done?' his voice was a low hiss.

'Tom, please,' she started.

His hand shot out, grabbing her wrist, yanking her forward. Before she could even register it, she felt the sharp, cold edge of his belt buckle striking her on the side of the head, the force of his fist in her chest knocking the air from her lungs. Her vision blurred with tears and pain as he swung again. She felt her knees give way, her mind spiralling as the blows were repeated, painting the hallway in streaks of her agony.

'You let strangers think I'm some kind of monster, is that it?' he shouted, his voice harsh and venomous.

'I di—'

'Do you have any idea what you've done?'

The words faded in and out as she crumpled against the wall, her body curling defensively, her senses retreating to a dull, muffled haze. Just before darkness took her, she caught a fleeting thought, a wish for escape.

When she finally came to, she found herself in the kitchen, slumped in a chair. She couldn't remember how she'd got there, but the room was dim, the faint evening light casting shadows across Tom's face as he sat opposite her, watching. Her head throbbed, her body ached all over, and as she shifted, pain radiated through her, sharp and insistent. She tried to lift her hand to touch her face, feeling something warm and sticky beneath her fingers. Her eyes drifted, searching the room, finally landing on Stevie's Captain Carrot toy lying abandoned in the corner. *Where's Stevie?* The question filled her mind, cutting through the haze of pain. Panic flared, sharp and immediate, but she kept her face as neutral as she could manage, blinking the blood out of her eye, trying to keep her breath even and shallow.

'Tom,' Her voice was barely more than a whisper, but he leaned forward, his face hard, unrelenting.

'You'll fix this, or I will,' he said coldly, his tone leaving no room for argument. He paused, his face twisting into a grimace.

'If you don't, Alison, I'll make sure you never see Stevie again. Do you understand me?'

The words sent a new wave of fear crashing over her, and she nodded, barely able to hold his gaze, a silent promise of compliance forming on her face. She felt her spine shrink under the weight of his words, the power that had risen in her shrunk back into the depths of her stomach. *No*, she whispered to herself.

After what felt like an eternity, he rose, leaving her in silence. She heard his heavy steps retreating down the hall. She didn't move, sitting in the dim light of the kitchen, swallowing down the wave of nausea that rose in her throat. She crossed the kitchen and clung to Captain Carrot, trying to steady herself, a single thought forming. *I must get us out of here.*

It was a thought she'd had a hundred times before, but this time, it felt different more desperate, more immediate, the rage burned in her stomach now. The power that had shrunk back in his presence was now a flicker of defiance that rumbled in her chest, burning to get out. She had been dormant for far too long. As she stood there, bruised and trembling, she made a vow to herself and to Stevie: *We will get out of here. And you will not get away with this.* The words burned within her, steady and unyielding, and they would not be extinguished.

▶II

In the weeks that followed, Tom became almost unrecognisable. He'd been apologetic, attentive, even gentle – a side of him that Alison hadn't seen in years. He looked after her, nursed her back to health, and made sure her wound was properly sutured. He made a show of fussing over her, reminiscing about the good old days, weaving promises that he'd never lay a hand on her again. But when Alison cautiously broached the subject of having the SoulLink removed, his demeanour shifted. The mask cracked, his face darkening, his warmth replaced with cold avoidance. He dodged the question entirely, and for a fleeting moment, she thought his temper might flare again. The air between them had grown taut, and she knew better than to push further. So, she played along, kept in his good books, careful to appear compliant. She smiled, nodded at his hollow promises, and let him believe that he had regained her trust. Beneath the surface, her resolve burned fiercer than ever. She would wait, bide her time and when the moment came, she would hit him, not with fists or rage, but with something far sharper. She would strike where it would hurt the most.

►II

Alison pulled herself upright, each movement slow and deliberate, wincing as her body protested with sharp, unwelcome reminders of the last two weeks. She made her way into Dr Anwar's office and lowered herself into the chair opposite, careful to mask any sign of discomfort. The bruises on her face had faded just enough to pass without question, and the lump on her head was hidden beneath her thick hair, but the pain lingered. She clenched her jaw and held herself steady, determined to keep any trace of what lay beneath from slipping to the surface. The room buzzed faintly with the hum of a heater kicking in, it was cold today – a good excuse to keep her coat on. When she spoke, her voice was quiet, carefully curated. She talked about her husband in fragments, skirting any details that might lead Dr Anwar to call the police. Alison couldn't afford that. It would mean being investigated, and with that, the system's cold, unblinking gaze would turn from her and begin to look at Stevie. She could already see it: social workers asking questions, evaluating her, evaluating Stevie, weighing her life in balance against Tom's charm, and his well-practised lies. He'd bring up Alison's mother, her 'episodes,' and paint her as unstable. *'Just like her mother,'* he'd say. The words would stick. They'd take Stevie, and the thought of it made Alison feel as if her life might stop.

Alison had grown up in care, bounced from house to house. She couldn't do that Stevie. Tom would be left unscathed, and she would be alone, at his mercy. He would relish the hunt, perhaps even kill her.

The rain had started again, soft against the window,

and she glanced out searching for an answer somewhere in the leaden sky. *How did it come to this?* She asked herself. *How did he turn from the man I loved into the man, I fear? Was he always like this?* The past five years unravelled in her mind, a mess of broken promises and creeping dread. *Had she been blind, or simply foolish?*

Dr Anwar's hand shifted across the desk, a small, folded note sliding into view. Alison's gaze moved to it, with a hint of apprehension. *I did some research on SoulLink*, the note read. She looked up, meeting Dr Anwar's steady gaze, and for the second time in the last three weeks she felt a spark of hope. She swallowed it down quickly, like poison, put her head down and read on. *SoulLink has hidden user settings they call 'vaults.' They're secure storage spaces within the device. Many men use them to stash away infidelities or save memories they don't want their spouses to see. Could you create your own vault, a private record of everything, stored safely out of his reach?*

The suggestion stirred something in Alison. It was dangerous, but it was a lifeline. She might be able to build proof without the risk of discovery, but her unease crept in. Tom had everything password protected. Every device, every account, all locked down behind his wall of paranoia and control. The thought of entering his study, sitting in his chair and touching his computer, felt like tempting a tiger and daring it to bite.

▶ll

Alison lay in bed that night, awake and motionless, her mind churning over Dr Anwar's words. The room was dark, the faint light from the street outside pooling in thin, cold lines along the walls. Tom lay beside her, breathing heavily. She closed her eyes, focusing on her breath, feeling each beat of her heart slowing, softening. In the silence, she slipped out of bed, taking care not to shift the mattress, and crept down the hall. Every floorboard seemed to stretch and groan beneath her feet, amplifying her steps. The door to Tom's study loomed before her and she paused, half expecting him to be there or to have followed quietly behind. She glanced over her shoulder as if he might appear out of the shadows. He didn't.

The door creaked softly as she eased it open, and the familiar smell of stale coffee and leather settled over her. She sank into his chair, her fingers tingling with adrenaline. Breathing deep, she suppressed her heart so that it didn't spike. The monitor cast a cold, blue light that made the walls seem to close in, and for a second, she thought she saw him in the dark window, ghostly and hollow-eyed, staring in from the cold. Her fingers moved over the keyboard, poised but trembling. She tried to guess his password. Her birthday, Stevie's, his mother's. But nothing worked. Each failed attempt sent a flicker of frustration and fear through her. She bit her lip, the urge to abandon it pulling at her. Her heartbeat began to quicken. If she was caught on the SoulLink app or locked out, the trail would lead straight back. She couldn't risk it. She stifled a sharp intake of breath and forced herself to breathe, steady, slow. She powered down the computer, carefully smoothing over any trace of her presence, then slipped back out of the office and into bed, her nerves on edge, buzzing with the bitter frustration. She couldn't stop now. There had to be another way.

In the days that followed, Alison watched Tom closely, studying him with new intensity. She observed him entering his office, memorising the pauses and glances that marked his careful process, noting the patterns he followed as he keyed in his password, the letters he hovered over. She pieced together fragments, analysing every detail like a puzzle she was desperate to solve. Yesterday, she had caught a glimpse of *eRo* on the screen and spent hours trying to decipher it, turning the letters over in her mind. That morning, after Tom left for work and she'd dropped Stevie off at school, she sat down at the kitchen table and began scribbling combinations on a scrap of paper. Her nerves were taut as she tried to focus. At 11:00 AM, a knock startled her. Alison stood, her heart skipping as she crossed the hallway. For a fleeting moment, she feared it might be Simon, the overly friendly postman whose harmless flirting had already gotten her in trouble, but she could see no sign of the red uniform or postal trolly through the glass. She braced herself and pulled the door open.

It wasn't Simon. It was Jen.

Relief and guilt crashed over Alison in equal measure.

'Hi, Ally,' Jen said softly, her voice warm but cautious.

'Oh, Jen,' she whispered, her voice breaking. 'It's so lovely to see you.'

Alison reached out, wrapping her arms around Jen, clinging to her like a drowning dog finding solid ground. Taken aback by Alison's sudden embrace, Jen steadied herself and followed her to the kitchen. Jen sat down as Alison busied herself making tea, her hands moving too quickly, in a display of nervousness.

'You know,' Jen began, her tone cautious but firm, 'This isn't the first time I've popped round. I've been here a few times over the weekend, and Tom told me you were either unwell or away with Stevie.'

Alison froze for a moment, gripping the edge of the counter. The anger rose hot and fast inside her, threatening to spill over. Of course, Jen had been round. Alison straightened herself, willing her face into a neutral expression, though her voice was tight.

'I think he might've got it wrong,' she said, trying to sound calm. 'Or maybe. . . maybe he was just trying to protect me.'

Jen's eyes narrowed, disbelief flickering across her face.

'Protect you?' she said slowly, 'Ally, I saw him in a bar a little while ago. He called me a slut, told me you'd said I slept with the boss to get my promotion.'

The words hung in the air like a slap, and Alison felt

her stomach churn. Of course, Tom had said something. It was exactly what he said he'd do if she went back to her old job. He'd done it to isolate her, to tarnish even her most steadfast friendships. Jen's voice softened, but there was an edge to it, a mix of hurt and determination.

'I've been over twice in the last two weeks, but Tom's always been here. I took the afternoon off work to pop round today, and I'm glad I did. You look... well, you don't look like yourself.'

Alison turned away, staring into the steaming cups of tea, her hands gripping the counter so tightly her knuckles whitened. The weight of Tom's manipulations pressed on her.

'Jen... I'm glad you came, and I did say that,' Alison admitted, her voice tight, 'but it was just a silly joke. I didn't mean anything by it. I was jealous of your promotion. . . stuck at home changing nappies while you were moving up in the world. God, I missed you. And I'm fine, honestly, just having trouble sleeping.'

'Hey, you still got that SoulLink thing in?' she asked, her tone light though the question was serious.

'No,' Alison replied quickly, nodding even as the word left her mouth.

'I'm glad you got rid of it. You know, loads of women have come forward lately, talking about how it's ruined their lives. Husbands using it to track every little thing, every thought. It's mad, they. . .'

Alison held up a hand to stop her, forcing a small laugh.

'Yep, as I said, I got rid of it ages ago. So, it's just me here now.'

Her pulse quickened, and she tried to keep her expression neutral. Jen's face shifted, a mix of confusion and pity. Alison leaned forward, scribbling on a scrap of paper. *He could be listening*, it read. Jen's eyes darted to the note, and she quickly changed the subject.

'So, how's Stevie getting on at school? How have you been since your mum passed?'

'Did he tell you?' she asked quietly.

'I came round to ask when the service was, but Tom said you were busy. He never got back to me.'

Alison swallowed hard, the memory of the lonely day washing over her.

'It was just family,' she lied, her voice hollow.

She thought of how much she had wished for someone to sit beside her, to share in the grief. Jen squeezed Alisons hand.

Over the next hour, the conversation shifted, the two women slipping into memories of old times, a bittersweet warmth filling the room. They laughed about their carefree years, about pranks and late - night chats, until the topic of work came up.

'Have you thought about going back?' Jen asked, her tone cautious. Alison smiled faintly, the kind that didn't quite reach her eyes.

'I'd love to, but. . . I'll have to think about it. And speak to Tom.'

Jen raised an eyebrow but didn't press further. Alison walked Jen to the door, reluctant to let her go. They lingered there, staring at each other, something unspoken passing between them. Before Jen stepped off the porch, she slipped a small piece of paper into Alison's hand.

'Call me,' she said softly, her voice steady but her eyes brimming with concern. Alison nodded, clutching the slip of paper tightly against her palm.

▶ll

When Alison returned home after picking Stevie up, Tom was waiting in the kitchen. His posture was rigid, eyes cold, and Alison braced herself for the interrogation. He was angry, that much was clear, but there was something restrained in his demeanour, likely the memory of the beating he had dealt out just two weeks ago. It was fresh enough to keep him cautious, tempering his rage, though not by much.

'What was she doing here?' He snapped, his voice low but sharp cutting through the silence. 'Why were you talking to that slut? What did she want? Why didn't you call me to let me know she was coming round?'

The questions came fast, each one laced with accusation, each one aimed at Alison. He loomed over her, relentless, his anger bubbling.

'She was concerned,' Alison said evenly, her voice calm, careful. 'She just wanted to chat. It was nice to see her.'

'Oh, nice, was it? Nice?' He sneered, pacing now. 'Going to get married, are they?' He paused, glaring. 'What else did she want? Did you tell her you'd go to the wedding? Did you say you'd go back to work? Why didn't you talk to me about this? Have you been keeping things from me?'

The barrage of questions came one after another, his tone growing darker with each. Alison stood her ground, careful to keep her breathing steady, her expression neutral. She answered every question with deliberate calm, her voice betraying neither fear nor irritation. Each response was measured, devoid of malice.

'Yes, we talked. She came round because she was concerned. Yes, we talked about the past. No, I didn't say I'd go back to work. I told her I had to speak to you first.'

She kept her tone light, even, as if his words were just another conversation but beneath the surface, something inside Alison was shifting. Jen had seen her, spoken to her, heard her. Tom's questions rolled off her like water on stone. She saw through his anger for what it truly was: fear. He was losing his grip on her, and he knew it. Alison felt a flicker of power. Jen knew. Jen cared. And Tom could do nothing about it.

She moved past him, placing Stevie's bag on the counter and starting to unpack it. Tom stood there for a moment, seething, his fury trying to find a foothold. Alison glanced at him, a small, controlled smile on her lips.

'I'll pop dinner on,' she said softly, her tone free of the tension that usually laced her every word to him. She felt steady, in control of herself.

Tom left the room, but she could feel the weight of his frustration lingering. As Alison set about preparing dinner, the embers of defiance smouldered quietly in her chest. Today didn't feel like enduring. She was planning, and Tom's control was beginning to slip.

▶︎❙❙

The following morning, Alison moved around the kitchen with careful precision, her mind running over the fragments she'd gathered in recent weeks. As Tom leaned against the counter, distracted, his fingers moved quickly over the keyboard of his laptop. She glanced up, just briefly, catching a glimpse of the screen as he typed. It wasn't much, just a few more letters, but something clicked. *C feRo.* She froze for the briefest of moments, then turned back to the sink, her hands trembling as she scrubbed at an already-clean plate. *CafeRouge.* Their first date. Of course it would be something sentimental, a relic of the man he pretended be. She moved through the rest of the morning on autopilot, masking her triumph with a neutral expression, forcing herself not to think about what came next.

That evening, she crushed two sleeping pills into Tom's dinner. He ate without suspicion, grumbling about work, Stevie's school, and a dozen other petty grievances that barely registered with her. She nodded along, murmuring agreement, her mind fixed on what she needed to do. By the time they had gone to bed Tom had begun to slur his words, his eyelids drooping. When the house had finally settled into silence, she rose from the bed, heart rate steady and her steps as light as air. She crept to Tom's study, opened the door and eased into the chair, fingers trembling as she typed *CafeRouge* into the password field, and exhaled when the screen unlocked. Her fingers moved quickly, navigating to the SoulLink dashboard. The sight made her stomach churn.

His control centre was laid out before her, a stark reminder of how deeply he'd invaded her life. The dashboard was cluttered with folders, dozens, maybe hundreds, each one a collection of her most private thoughts, her moments of pain, fear, and even joy, catalogued for his amusement. She forced herself not to linger, not to look too deeply. Her eyes caught on a file name that made her blood run cold: *Ally's Fantasies.* She recoiled, stung by the shame, bile rising in her throat. Those thoughts had been hers and only hers. He had no right to them. She clenched her fists, forcing the anger back, focusing on the task at hand. She moved quickly now, a mixture of urgency and defiance propelling her forward. She took out her phone, logged into the SoulLink app, and synced it to his account. With each tap of the screen, she configured the hidden vault, proof of his cruelty and control. Tomorrow she would upload the memory data files, while he was at work.

When the setup was complete, she methodically erased every trace of her activity, wiping the computer clean. Satisfied, she shut it down, eased the chair back into place, and slipped out of the study, closing the door softly behind her.

Back in bed, Alison lay still, breathing steady, her mind whirring. Tomorrow, she would put the plan into action and begin the painstaking process of archiving her memories. She would collect the evidence she needed, piecing together a picture of Tom that no one else had seen. The monster behind the charming facade.

►||

Alison waited until the door slammed shut and Tom's heavy footsteps faded. Her heart steadied the moment she heard his car pull away. She retrieved her phone from the kitchen counter and slipped into the bedroom, her hands trembling as she opened the SoulLink app. The hidden vault was an empty void, waiting for her to fill it with all she had endured. She took a breath, her finger hovering over the screen before selecting *Upload Memory Data,* making quick work of recalling events. Memories of the last three years surged to the forefront of her mind as she watched them play out, the arguments, the violence, bruises hidden under makeup, Stevie's scared eyes witnessing too much. Her jaw clenched as she relived each memory, carefully selecting fragments and methodically transferring the worst years of her life into a vault. Every memory she uploaded felt like a small victory. When the archive was complete, she renamed the folder: *Download Me*. She took the scrap of paper Jen had passed to her, copied the email address, and wrote a simple subject line: Just in case. In the message to Jen, she typed one line. *Wait for my signal. Don't write back, just download.* She deleted the message, erasing her tracks. She stared at the piece of paper Jen had given her, just a name an email and a small note. *I'm here if you need me.*

▶‖

Jen's Inbox chimed as she sat at her desk sipping her mid-morning coffee, her fingers hovering over the mouse as she sensed the weight behind Alison's message. The subject line alone, *Just in case,* caught her attention.

Without hesitation she clicked the download link. Jen's breath caught in her throat. Alison's face filled the screen, bruised, anguished, her lip swollen. Tom's words came like daggers degrading her, accusations and insults thrown alongside the plates and furniture he hauled at her. Alisons voice cut through, placating him and apologising. Jen paused the video, tears pricked her eyes. She couldn't stop now. She owed it to Alison to continue. With a shaking hand she pressed play and continued to the next file and the next. The recordings played as Jen sat frozen, listening to the accusations and insults as Stevie's quiet sobs punctuated every image. She watched in horror, the stark truth of Alison's life spilling onto her screen. A lump formed in Jen's throat as she scrolled through each memory forcing herself to experience Alison's pain.

She sat back, anger and sadness twisting in her chest. *How had she not seen this? How had things gotten so bad?* Her jaw set with steely determination, she opened her desk drawer and took out a memory stick and copied the files over quickly, the tiny device filling with everything Alison had risked her life to share. Jen's resolve hardened. *He will not get away with this.*

▶❙❙

Alison sat at the kitchen table, her phone buzzing softly beside her as Stevie finished her dinner. She picked it up absentmindedly, scrolling through notifications when one caught her eye: *'Go live with SoulLink! Share your day in real time.'* Her stomach twisted at the idea, but a spark of determination ignited the flame. She opened the notification, navigating through the prompts. Her fingers hovered over the date selector, and she carefully set it: *Saturday 17 November, 2:00 PM*, two days from now. Their wedding anniversary. She clicked *Accept Terms and Conditions*, her hands steady despite the adrenaline coursing through her veins. The app confirmed the setup, linking the SoulLink Node to her newly reactivated Facebook account. She sent an email to Jen with the Subject: *Facebook Saturday, 17*

November, 2:00 PM and deleted the evidence.

Alison carried Stevie into the living room.

'Paw Patrol, okay?' she said, brushing her hair gently.

Stevie nodded, her little face lighting up at the familiar theme song. Alison kissed her head and went back to the kitchen, her mind already on edge. She plated Tom's dinner carefully, arranging and rearranging the food nervously. When Tom arrived home, she greeted him with a warm smile and handed him the plate. He looked around, pleased. The house was spotless, Stevie was quiet, and dinner was ready. For now, he was satisfied. He sat at the table, eating in silence while Alison kept herself busy. She scrubbed dishes, wiped down counters, anything to appear occupied, ordinary.

Alison's phone buzzed, the faint vibration cutting through the quiet. Tom picked it up before she could reach for it, his eyebrows furrowing.

'What's this?' he asked, holding the phone up. Her heart stopped for a moment, but she forced the feeling down, squashing it.

'Oh, it's probably spam,' she said lightly, turning back to the sink.

'You still have the app?' he said unconvinced. His tone sharp now.

'I thought I got rid of it; it must not have registered,' she turned; her expression carefully neutral, took the phone from him, opening the app to show him. 'See?'

Tom's face darkened as he swiped through the app. Each tap felt like a test, daring her to react. She had spent hours ensuring the vault was invisible, leaving the account devoid of anything incriminating. Just today's memory, streaming into Tom's cloud account straight from her consciousness. She stood frozen to the spot breathless while she waited.

'There's nothing here,' he muttered, his suspicion still simmering.

'Exactly,' she said softly, keeping her voice calm. 'If it bothers you, just delete it.'

Alison paused, feeling emboldened. Or maybe we should get rid of them. We don't use them anymore, do we?' Tom hesitated, still scrolling. The suggestion disarming him enough to temper his anger. He tapped the phone, muttering under his breath before tossing it onto the counter.

'Don't do anything stupid, Alison,' he warned.

She nodded, picking the phone up as if nothing had happened. Her nerves screamed, but she remained composed. She kept her movements light, her breathing steady as Tom returned to his plate. He may have been suspicious, but he hadn't found anything.

▶∥

The morning of 17 November began like any other, with Alison moving through the house in near silence, her eyes darting to the clock as the minutes ticked by. When Tom finally rose, she greeted him with warmth and set out a light breakfast, plating it neatly in front of him and making casual conversation while he ate, her smile soft but practiced. He ate without much conversation, and when he retreated to get ready for the day, Alison turned her attention to Stevie. She crouched in front of her daughter, brushing the hair from her face.

'You're going to have a lovely day with Auntie Jen, sweetheart,' she whispered.

As Alison grabbed the car keys, preparing to take Stevie, Tom appeared in the hallway, his presence filling the space with unease. His eyes narrowed, his suspicion immediate.

'Where are you going?'

'It was supposed to be a surprise, Jen asked me if she could have Stevie for the day,' Alison replied smoothly.

'Why didn't you tell me? I don't like surprises,' Tom's jaw tightened, his eyes narrowing as he stepped closer.

'I didn't think it was a big deal. I thought we could enjoy a quiet afternoon,' she said, her voice even, her grip on the car keys tightening.

Tom stared her down, his silence stretching unbearably.

Then he shook his head, his lips curling into a grim line.

'No. Stevie stays here, and you're not going anywhere.'

Alison hesitated, her mind racing. For a moment, she thought about insisting, but the warning in his eyes stopped her. It wasn't time yet. She gave a small, appeasing nod, her voice calm.

'Of course, Tom. If that's what you want.'

He gave a satisfied grunt, moving past her toward the living room. Alison stood there for a moment, her hands gripping the car keys tightly before placing them back on the counter. Her plans had shifted, unravelling under Tom's watchful eye, but she would adapt. She had to for Stevie's sake. From the living room, Stevie's laughter rose above the cheerful voices of her cartoons, piercing the heavy quiet that had settled over Alison. It was a sound so free and happy, it made her chest ache.

Alison stepped out into the garden. The bitter cold had stripped the trees and only a few solitary branches held on to the yellowing leaves. She reached for the broom, sweeping the fallen ones into small piles, her movements mechanical. Alison had loved this garden when they had first moved in, she had poured herself into it, pruning and planting new life. Stevie was nearly three, and Alison realised with a pang of guilt that her daughter had never planted a single seed, had never felt the dirt between her small fingers. She thought about what her mother had taught her, that she might teach Stevie. Looking out over the garden at the piles of leaves scattered across the soil she exhaled a breath that carried years of grief. *Three more hours*, she reminded herself. *Just three more hours*. She picked up the broom again, the scrape of bristles against the stone path grounding her in the moment. The sun shifted behind a cloud, casting a grey pall over the garden, but Alison didn't stop. She would plant seeds with Stevie, teach her to nurture life.

Tom ate with his usual distracted indifference while Alison kept the conversation flowing just enough to keep him at ease. Stevie was settled with her lunch in the living room and so she made herself busy, clearing food away, refilling his glass, all the while glancing at the clock. Casually, she mentioned wanting to go back to work. She saw the flicker of irritation in his face but pressed no further. Then, while tidying the table, she mentioned Jen again, her voice light, almost playful. Her heart pounded, but outwardly she remained calm. She checked on Stevie once more and closed the doors between the living room and kitchen. Alison returned to the table and sat across from him. She had been careful to place Tom's phone face down on the counter as she worked, her movements deliberate. Now, with her hands folded neatly in her lap, she looked at the clock. It was 2:00 PM.

'I need to talk to you about something,' she said, her voice calm, measured.

'What is it?' he replied glancing up. She had his attention.

▶II

Jen logged onto her computer and opened Facebook, leaving the tab active while she pottered around, glancing occasionally to see if Alison might pop up. A notification pinged. 'Alison Bryant and Tom Bryant will be sharing their big day soon,' Jen frowned, the message catching her off guard. She had heard about this SoulLink feature but had never actually seen it used, aside from the viral videos of overly ambitious proposals or awkward conscious live streams that had made the rounds online. She'd laughed at those once, but this was different. Alison Bryant was married. What big day? Jen thought. Her chest tightened. This had to be Alison's signal. *But what did it mean? What was about to happen?*

At exactly 2:00 PM, another notification came through. 'Alison Bryant is now streaming live. Join her on her big day!' Jen's heart leapt into her throat. The window opened on her desktop, buffering for a brief moment before it loaded a livestream from Alisons kitchen. Tom's face appeared, his expression twisted with fury, his body tense. Alison was there too; she could hear her. Jen stared, her stomach knotting as Tom's voice cut through the static. This wasn't just a signal. It was something far bigger, far darker. Jen gripped the edges of her desk, unable to look away.

'I need to talk to you about something,' it was Alison, her voice calm and measured.

Tom glanced up, narrowing his eyes. 'What is it?'

'I want a divorce.'

The words hung in the air, a loaded silence stretching between them.

The comments began to come in.

Heartless!

How could she do this?

Poor Tom, does he know this is streaming?

For a moment, Tom just stared into the camera, his expression blank, as if he couldn't quite process what she'd said. Then his face twisted, his hand slamming down on the table with a force that made the glasses rattle.

'You want a what?' he hissed, his voice low, dangerous.

Go Tom! One of his gym buddies wrote.

'I want a divorce,' Alison repeated, her voice steady despite the tremor in her chest. 'I can't do this anymore, Tom.'

Tom erupted. He shoved his chair back, the legs screeching against the floor as he stood, towering over her. His words came in a torrent of venom, accusatory. She had betrayed him, she was ungrateful, trying to ruin his life.

'You think you can just leave me?' he screamed, stepping closer. 'You don't get to decide! After everything I've done for you!'

His hand lashed out before Alison could respond, striking her across the face with enough force that it knocked her sideways. The comment began like a flurry as their friends and family watched and more people joined the livestream.

What's going on?

I can't see anything.

Did he just hit her?

Does anyone know where they live?

Is this real?!

Call the police, someone call the police!

Oh my God, Tom, stop!

▶❚❚

Alison gasped, her head ringing, but this time something inside her snapped. For years, Alison had absorbed his blows, had shrunk beneath his control, but now, now, something was different. As he lunged at her again, she pushed back, her hands finding purchase on his chest and shoving him away with all her strength.

'Don't touch me!' she screamed, her voice filled with a defiance she hadn't felt in years.

Tom stumbled, caught off guard by her resistance. He grabbed her arm, yanking her toward him, but Alison fought harder. She clawed at his face, her nails digging into his flesh, survival instincts kicking in.

'You're done, Tom!' she spat, her voice trembling but fierce. 'You don't own me!'

The live stream reached a growing audience as people shared the video across their profiles and messaging groups. The comment section filled with a chaotic mix of outrage and disbelief.

Can you believe this, she told him she wanted it to be over and now she might get what she asked for? Laughing emoji, crying laughing emoji.

He's kickin the crap outta her?

What's going on?

Did she cheat? Did he cheat?

Why is no one taking this seriously, someone call the police!!!!

Alison felt the sharp sting of his fists, the dull ache

of her body colliding with the table, but she refused to stop. She kicked, scratched, shoved, anything to keep him from gaining the upper hand. Tom's rage was like a wildfire, consuming everything in its path, but Alison's defiance only stoked his desperation. She caught glimpses of his face, wild, red, panicked as though he could sense his control had slipped through his fingers. Then, somewhere in the chaos, he stepped back, his chest heaving, his face twisted in fury and disbelief. Alison stood across from him, blood trickling from her lip, her breath coming in ragged gasps, but she didn't back down.

'I'm done, Tom. You're not going to hurt me again,' she said, her voice raw but unwavering.

Tom clenched his fists, his body trembling with suppressed rage, but he didn't move toward her, flashing blue lights filtered through the kitchen window. His face contorted with a fresh wave of anger as he realised what was happening. The police were on the driveway, alerted by the flood of calls from horrified viewers who had seen him for what he was. Tom stood, his breath heaving, his knuckles bloodied. Alison slid down the cupboards onto the floor, her resolve burning even brighter despite the pain. The door burst open, and two officers stormed in, pulling Tom away from Alison as he shouted protests.

'You've got it all wrong!' he wailed. 'This is a misunderstanding! I've never done this before! I just lost control.'

The officers didn't reply, their faces impassive as they cuffed him.

'You don't understand!' Tom continued, his voice cracking. 'Check the SoulLink! Check her memories there's nothing there! Nothing but love!'

An officer turned to Alison.

'Are you okay, ma'am?'

Alison nodded faintly, wincing as she tried to sit up. She gestured to the bookshelf where her phone sat recording.

'The feed,' she whispered. 'It's all there.'

The officer followed her gaze, nodding to his partner, who retrieved the phone and carefully powered it down. Alison sagged back against the wall in exhaustion. The world around her blurred before the sound of distant voices outside pulled her back. Tom was led out to the waiting police car, his hands cuffed behind his back, his protests loud.

'You've got it all wrong!' he shouted.

Jen stepped forward from the curb, her hand clenching a small memory stick. Her knuckles were white, her body vibrating with fear and anger. Her voice was firm when she spoke.

'I think you'll want to see this,' she said, handing it to the officer in the nearest car.

Tom's head snapped around, his face twisting with rage, eyes burning with fury as he locked on Jen.

'You interfering slut!' he spat. 'This is your fault!'

Jen didn't flinch. She stared back at him, her jaw set,

her gaze unwavering. 'I'll take that as a compliment,' she said coldly, watching as the officers shoved him into the back seat. His protests were muffled as the door slammed shut.

The moment the car pulled away, the tension in Jen's body seemed to melt, her knees wobbling slightly as she exhaled. Without missing a beat, she turned and rushed toward the house.

Inside, Alison sat propped up against the kitchen cabinets, her face swollen and lip split. Stevie was being comforted by a policewoman nearby, her little hands clutching Captain Carrot. The girl's eyes were wide, but she wasn't crying. She stared at her mother with concern as Jen sat beside Alison.

'What an afternoon, aye?'

Alison managed a weak laugh.

'Don't,' she murmured, her voice hoarse. 'It hurts too much to laugh.'

Alison looked at Jen, her bloodshot eyes glistening

with unshed tears.

'Thank you,' she whispered. 'For everything.'

'You don't have to thank me,' Jen said softly, pulling Alison into a gentle hug. 'That's what friends are for, right? We've always been there for each other.'

She hesitated, her voice cracking slightly. 'But I should have seen this. I should have known how bad it was.'

Alison shook her head weakly.

'I was so wrapped up in my own world, I missed the signs. And I've been replaying everything in my head, trying to figure out how this happened.'

'If *I* couldn't see it, how were *you* meant to?' Jen looked at Alison forlorn and shook her head.

'I don't know,' she said. 'I don't know.'

Alison pressed her forehead lightly against Jen's shoulder. For a few moments, neither of them spoke. The weight of guilt, grief, and relief settled between them Jen lifted her head and cupped Alison's face gently.

'But here's what I *do* know,' she said 'You're not alone anymore. We'll figure this out. Together.'

▶ ||

The morning light filtered softly through the blinds as Alison sat at her kitchen table. The faint bruises on her face had faded to yellow, and the scab on the back of her neck where the SoulLink had almost healed. She sighed deeply, a mix of relief and lingering grief. It had been two weeks since Tom's arrest, and while her body was healing, her heart still carried the weight of everything. But the air in her home felt lighter, the walls less suffocating, and every moment that passed was hers. She took off her Fitbit, the last reminder of Tom's constant surveillance, and dropped it into the bin. Outside, Stevie giggled on the porch, her laughter carrying through the open window. Jen stood nearby, keeping an eye on her while sipping tea. When Jen stepped inside, she greeted Alison with a warm hug.

'You're looking better already,' Jen said, sincerity in

her tone.

'Thanks,' Alison replied, a small smile breaking through. 'Feels good to just. . . breathe.'

Stevie darted into the house, grabbing a sandwich from the table before running back outside. Alison poured another two cups of tea and led Jen back into the garden, where the winter sun cast a pale light over the empty flower beds.

'Do you ever feel. . . scared?' Jen asked gently, her voice cautious. Alison considered the question, glancing at Stevie as she played in the distance.

'I do,' she admitted. 'But I've got Stevie, and I've got you.'

'To moving forward,' Jen said, raising her cup in a small toast.

'To moving forward,' Alison echoed, raising her own.

She looked out over the garden, her eyes drifting until they landed on Stevie, clutching Captain Carrot in her little hands. A smile surfaced on her face, warm and hopeful.

'What shall we plant first?' said Alison, playfully.

'Carrots!' Shouted Stevie, 'Lots and lots of carrots!'

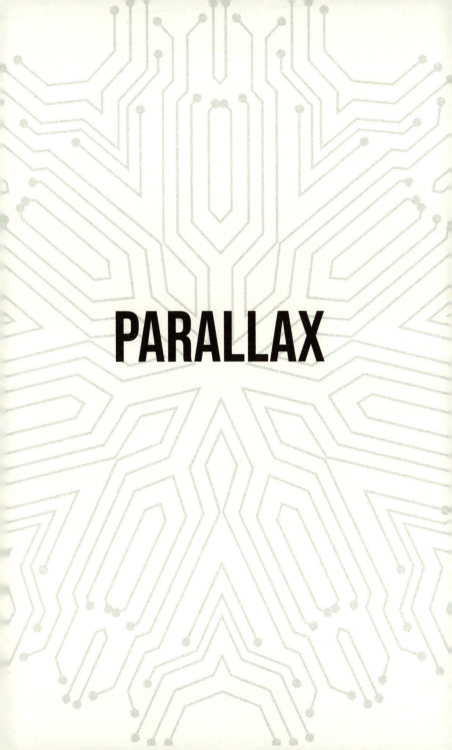
PARALLAX

PARALLAX

PARALLAX

The woman sat on the curb outside the police station, arms wrapped tightly around her knees as if holding herself together. It was 4:00 AM, the dead hour, when the living slept. As the sky expanded to the colour of a deep bruise, the first light of dawn bled into the horizon, casting long shadows. Slicks of oil on the road turned into rainbow blotches that shimmered and swirled like something alive. She stared at one as it caught the light, losing herself in its hypnotic dance until a voice interrupted the stillness.

'Freya, is it?'

The words were soft but had an edge. Freya blinked, slowly dragging her eyes upward. Standing before her was a soft-featured small woman. Freya's eyes, glassy and rimmed with exhaustion, struggled to focus.

'I'm Sam,' the woman crouched slightly, her voice pitched low and careful. 'I'm with the Cambridgeshire Police. You called about an assault. A sexual assault.' Sam pressed on as Freya stared vacantly. 'We'd like to take you somewhere we can talk. It's not far from here. Would that be okay?'

Freya nodded, the movement sluggish, her head bobbing as if too heavy for her neck. Her eyes were raw and bloodshot, tiny red threads spidered across her cheeks and neck. A chill ran through Sam, and it wasn't just the morning air. Freya looked like someone who'd had her neck wrung; her body trembled as Sam helped her to her feet.

The walk to the car was silent except for the shuffle of Freya's shoes against the pavement. Sam kept a steady grip on her arm, trying to gauge whether the tremors were from fear or the cold. Maybe both.

When they reached the car, Grant was already there, standing by the back door like a scarecrow that came to life. He still had that bright-eyed, eager look that hadn't yet been dimmed by years on the job.

'This is my colleague, Grant,' Sam said as they approached. 'We work together. Grant, this is Freya.'

'Hi, Freya,' Grant said.

Freya's gaze flickered to him and then to the back seat. She hesitated when she saw the plastic sheet stretched over the upholstery.

'It's just something we do,' Grant said gently. 'It helps keep any evidence safe, that's all. You don't need to worry about it, I promise.'

Freya didn't respond. Her eyes lingered on the plastic for a beat too long before she slid into the car without a word. She caught Sam exchanging a glance with Grant as she closed the door behind her, and her mind began to race. Why was she even here? Would they believe her? What would happen if they spoke to people at her workplace – or worse, if they talked to *him*?

A fresh jolt of panic tightened her chest, and she shifted uncomfortably, her body coiling like a spring, ready to leap the moment the car stopped. Her fingers gripped the door handle so tightly her knuckles turned white; she knew running wouldn't do her any good – not in this state.

Sam's hand gently covered hers. 'It's going to be okay,' she said, her voice a gentle tether.

Freya's grip on the handle loosened as she let out a shaky breath, swallowing hard. She didn't reply. Instead, she turned to face the window, her reflection staring back at her. For the rest of the drive, she avoided Sam's gaze, afraid that one more look of kindness from this woman might be the thing to unravel her completely.

When they arrived at the crisis centre, a woman was waiting for them by the doorway. She had kind eyes that seemed to see straight through Freya. Her look, so sympathetic, made something inside Freya twist uncomfortably – she was reminded of the way the vet had looked at her when her cat had been put to sleep. That quiet, measured pity. Freya wanted to scream, to shove it all away, but her body betrayed her. She collapsed into the woman's arms, clutching her desperately as the weight she'd been carrying finally tore her down. Her body heaved with sobs and relief as she gave way to the grief and the violation. But the solace was fleeting – the numbness that had shielded her was giving way to a wave of pain and anguish she wasn't ready to face.

'I can't. I can't,' she murmured, her voice trembling.

The woman's voice remained calm and reassuring. 'Freya, it's okay. You've survived this. Just a little more to go. You've done the right thing, and we don't have to talk about it unless you're ready.'

The woman supported her as she clung to her arms before introducing herself. 'My name is Joanna. I'm a crisis worker here at Haven, a dedicated centre for sexual assault.'

Freya winced at the words, but Joanna pressed on with care. 'I'll be with you the entire time to help you understand what's happening. If you feel uncomfortable at any stage, we'll stop. This will be led by you. It'll go at your pace. Shall we head through?' Joanna gestured towards the hallway.

Freya hesitated before nodding. She felt Joanna's hand gently guiding her forward, and she followed, the weight of what lay ahead pressing down on her shoulders. As she entered the room, Joanna stopped the detectives at the door.

'The Forensic Nurse Examiner will be here shortly.' she said firmly. 'I think it would be best if it was women only from here,' Her tone left no room for argument.

Grant hesitated for a moment before nodding, a flicker

of awkwardness flushing his face. He gave Joanna a small, playful salute.

'I'll get some tea,' he said, retreating down the hallway.

As the door closed behind him, Sam unwrapped a sterile packet, pulling out a swab. 'Alright, Freya, I'm just going to take a quick swab from your mouth while Grant sorts you out a cuppa.'

Freya nodded, her compliance quiet and measured. She opened her mouth, and Sam gently moved the cotton swab inside, her eyes scanning Freya's face for evidence.

Freya slipped her arms out of the green shift dress her husband Matt had bought her five years ago. It had come from her favourite thrift shop, the one they always visited during their summer days in Cornwall. Only yesterday, she had cherished it; so many memories were woven into the fabric. But now it hung limp in her hands, lifeless, as if the love had been wrung out of it. Freya hesitated for a moment, her fingers brushing the delicate satin hem before she folded it carefully and slipped it into the evidence bag.

Freya watched as her personal belongings were carefully collected, each item slipped into transparent bags as if they were part of a packed lunch. The bright overhead light left her feeling exposed and vulnerable. The sterile glow illuminated every inch of her as the nurse worked methodically, taking swabs and collecting small particles with tweezers. She winced as the camera flashed, capturing intimate parts of her body she had never intended anyone to see. Not like this. Her shame clung to her like a second skin, and her body ached with the effort of holding herself together.

When the examination finally ended, Freya was led to the shower. The nurse stepped out, leaving her alone at last. She undressed quickly and dipped her head into the downpour, as the water cascaded over her, she felt a faint sense of herself returning. The hot water and soap stung, but she welcomed the sensation, twisting the tap further towards the red. The rising heat scalded her scalp and chest, but she didn't flinch. Instead, she absorbed it and scrubbed, working the soap into a lather as she dragged the sponge over herself again and again, determined to erase every trace of the night from her body. When she finally shut off the water, thick clouds of steam filled the room, clinging to the mirror and the walls. Freya stood for a moment, water dripping from her hair and her body, and stared at the foggy reflection. She didn't recognise the woman staring back at her. But at least she felt clean. At least she felt something.

Sam stood up as DI Charles Ginsburg appeared at the end of the hallway, her coat hanging off her shoulders, her usually composed face etched with panic. She looked dishevelled, undone, the energy of someone who had just come off a double shift.

'Excuse me, you can't go in there!' a nurse called out from behind.

'It's okay, she's with us,' Sam called back. The nurse

hesitated, her lips pursed into a tight line, before giving a curt nod and retreating back to her desk.

Sam shifted her stance, positioning herself squarely in the middle of the corridor like a goalkeeper guarding a net. Her body language was clear – no one was getting past without her say-so.

'Charles, look at me,' Sam said, her eyes trying to catch her colleague's.

'Is she okay?' Charles demanded, barely hearing Sam as she moved to push past, her attention locked on the door at the end of the corridor.

'No, Charles. *Look at me*,' Sam repeated, sharper now, her words cutting through the fog of Charles's panic.

Charles froze mid-step, finally meeting Sam's gaze. Her expression was tight, her back up. 'Just tell me,' she said. 'I can handle it.'

Sam exhaled slowly, keeping her tone even. 'She's in the shower at the moment. You can't go in.'

'Did she say who it was? Who did this to her?' Charles asked, her voice trembling with urgency, the rage simmering just beneath the surface.

'Yes,' Sam replied, holding her colleague's gaze. 'And he'll be arrested as soon as we have her statement.'

Charles's jaw tightened and she tried to move past Sam again. This time, it was Grant who stepped forward, his hand closing firmly around her arm. He tugged her back just enough to stop her momentum and meet her eyes.

'She's in the shower,' Grant said earnestly, his voice steady but laced with concern. 'The forensic nurse has done her job, but Charles. . . she's not okay. She's been hurt, badly. She doesn't look like herself right now. We just want to prepare you.'

Sam gave Grant a quick nod of approval and Charles stood frozen for a moment. She brushed away tears that were forming with the back of her hand as the torrent of emotions threatened to pull her under.

'Thanks,' Charles said quietly, her voice brittle but resolute. She drew in a deep, shaky breath, forcing herself to stand a little taller.

When Freya finally emerged, the room seemed to close in on itself. Damp hair clung to her face, her skin pink and raw from the scalding water. Charles was waiting. In an instant, all the detachment Freya had fought to hold onto dissolved, replaced by the crushing weight of what she had just washed away. It returned with brutal clarity; the stark cry that escaped Freya was raw and primal.

Charles rushed to her, pulling her into a fierce embrace. Together, they collapsed into each other, their grief overflowing and entwining as they sobbed. It was a grief that didn't belong to one person, a shared mourning for everything that had been irrevocably lost. They cried for Freya, they cried for Freya's husband, Matt; they cried for Freya's children and her mother and for their friendship; everything was different now. Like surviving cancer or the death of a parent, this was a before-and-after moment. Life would never be the same.

▶︎ ▌▌

The air of the police station was cold and sterile, its chill seeping into Freya's bones. Her skin prickled with gooseflesh, and she wrapped her arms tightly around herself, though it did little to ward off the sensation. She stood in the corridor, eyes wide and hollow; the weight of the last two months pressed down on her like a slab of stone. The pale morning light that filtered through the windows did nothing to lift the shadows in her mind.

She hadn't been to work since the incident. She knew, deep down, that if she ever returned, she could only avoid *him* for so long. The thought made her stomach churn. Around her, the muffled hum of distant voices mingled with the steady, insistent beat of her own heart, merging into a dissonant symphony of dread. *Why did I come here?* The question spun in her head, its edges sharp with nerves and shame. Her anger, once a blazing fire, had been replaced by something colder – doubt, fear, a gnawing helplessness.

She was taken from reception by a kind police officer and felt like a ghost drifting through the living as they reached a room where two detectives awaited her. One was her friend Charles, who gave her hand a squeeze; the other was DI Alice Morely, a straight-faced woman with a mask of professional concern.

Freya clenched her hands tightly in her lap, her knuckles white with tension and anger. In the corner of the room, the solitary camera blinked steadily, its unrelenting red eye fixed on her like a sniper tracking its target.

'Ms Sloane,' Alice spoke. She was wearing a stark suit and a white collar. '*He* has been offered leniency in exchange for cooperating.'

The detective leaned in slightly, her gaze steady but not unkind.

'It wasn't a decision made lightly,' she continued. 'The offer came from the Crown Prosecution Service once he agreed to provide names to help ongoing investigations.'

Alice paused, letting the words settle, then resumed with measured care.

'Other women from the firm have come forward. It's open knowledge there's something of a boys' club operating there,' her voice softened but she remained firm. 'I know this isn't easy, but with his cooperation, we can break it down. We can put the rest of them behind bars, where they belong.'

Silence filled the room. Across the table Charles shirted slightly, her gaze flickering to Alice then Freya as she tried to read her friend, waiting for the cracks to reveal themselves.

Freya sat frozen as the DI's words sank in, gnawing at her. She heard a faint, rhythmic bassline reverberating from somewhere beyond the walls. It was barely audible, but its presence was like a persistent itch under her skin, clinging to her like an unwelcome shadow she couldn't escape. Her fingers twitched involuntarily as the bassline swelled in her mind, growing louder and more persistent.

It rose like a wave, threatening to drag her under, pulling her back to the place she had fought so hard to leave behind. For two months, she had battled this memory, trying to suppress it, but now it surged forward, dragging her back to the room. The walls, bathed in a sickly red glow, seemed to pulse in time with the relentless beat.

Freya saw herself again, lying limp on the bed, limbs lifeless and eyes fixed on the flickering ceiling light above as it cast distorted shadows across the room. A figure loomed over, his face blurred and indistinct, but his presence terrifying, his satisfaction palpable. Freya couldn't move. Her body was unresponsive, like a marionette with its strings severed. Powerless. Trapped in a recurring nightmare, a fate she was now forced to relive over and over again.

The light above her flickered, this time more violently, again casting erratic shadows. The relentless music faltered for a moment, its rhythm stretching and distorting like a warped record. The walls closed in around her, vibrating with the pulsing beat, until suddenly, she snapped back to the harsh glare of the fluorescent lights in the interview room. Alice spoke again, her tone measured.

'Ms Sloane?'

'Dr Sloane or Freya,' she corrected, sharp like a blade.

'Freya, I'm sorry. We're on your side,' said the detective, her eyes softening just for a moment.

Charles leant forward and held Freya's hands, which trembled on the table. 'We're not here to rush you, Frey,' she said softly. 'We're here to listen. Whatever you need.'

Freya's eyes lifted to meet Charles's, searching her expression. Her warmth lingered, quieter, more grounded. For a second, she almost believed her. But the doubt was stronger. She knew how her friend could push her when it mattered, that her kindness was now a strategy. The thought knotted in her chest, and the faint throb of the bassline returned. She pulled her hands away and took a moment to calm her pounding heart, eyes closed. Then, her voice broke.

'Is there any point to this?'

The question hung in a silence that seemed to tell her everything she needed to know.

Alice answered first: 'You will give your extraction today. It will be shown in the court proceedings and go towards delaying his potential release.'

The tone had remained even, almost mechanical as if this part of the job was so familiar that she could switch onto autopilot to distance herself from it.

'But you said he might not face trial,' Freya's voice cracked now, the tears welling up in her eyes. 'If I give the extraction, I don't get to stare that bastard in the face.'

'It's best if it's not an emotional account. We need the facts,' the detective measured her words carefully. 'They'll see the extracted memory. It will be archived. If he does it again, it will be there, a permanent stain on his record.'

Freya's laugh was sharp as it cracked out of her.

'A stain,' she mustered, as though the past month had been nothing more than an inconvenient tea spill on an expensive Persian rug.

'Do you have any questions regarding the case?' Alice asked, attempting to steer the conversation back on track.

'When will he be released?' The words seemed to dissolve into the oppressive stillness of the room, almost as if she hadn't spoken at all.

'This is not something you should dwell on, Freya. I hear you're not talking to the therapist we assigned you.'

Freya stood abruptly, the chair scraping loudly against the floor, the anger bubbling in her chest.

'Fuck you!' she spat. 'I'm all talked out! Where has talking got me? My husband can't look at me – I can't even look at myself. And will *he* see it? Will *he*?'

'It's within his rights,' the detective replied, her tone still steady despite Freya's outburst. 'His lawyer has the right to review the evidence.'

'So, I give you my memory, and he gets to relive it?

It's sick!'

Freya slammed the door. Alice exchanged a glance with Charles, who quickly stood and followed her friend.

▶II

In the bathroom, Freya splashed cold water on her face. The sting of it sharp and real, bringing a fleeting moment of clarity from the chaos that swirled in her head. Then the memories surged forward like a tidal wave: the faceless man, the flickering ceiling light, her own body limp and unresponsive, moving like a ragdoll to the rhythm of her heart as it pounded in her chest. The soft creak of the bathroom door snapped her back to the present. Her eyes darted to the mirror, catching her own reflection – wide-eyed, red-rimmed – before turning to face Charles.

'Are you okay, Frey?' Charles's voice was soft but carried an edge of urgency.

Freya shot her a look of disbelief, her eyes laden with exhaustion and frustration. She shook her head, her lips pressed into a hard line.

Charles sighed and raised her hands slightly, a silent acknowledgment of the stupidity of her question.

'How is this happening?' Freya said finally. 'How can he just walk free?'

The tension between them softened, the bond of their friendship clear. Charles stepped closer and pulled Freya into a hug, her arms firm and reassuring. Freya didn't resist, she wanted reassurance, she wanted comfort, but her gaze dropped to the gun holster at Charles's side, her thoughts dark and churning.

'We'll get the bastard, Frey,' Charles murmured. 'Maybe not today, but we will. I promise you.'

Freya pulled back slightly, her face damp with tears.

Charles reached for a tissue and gently wiped them away, her expression steady, though her own eyes betrayed a flicker of sadness.

'You've just got to do this one last thing,' Charles said, her voice calm but resolute. 'Let them do the extraction. It needs to go on record.'

'What if it's hazy? What if it's not enough?' Freya hesitated, her voice trembling as her fears spilled out. 'What if they see something I've forgotten, or what if I have remembered it all wrong?'

Charles shook her head, speaking gently but firmly. 'We've gone over this. I know it's frightening, but, Frey, what have you got to lose?'

'It's not about what I lose, it's about what they gain! A fucking deep dive into my head. What are they going to see, Charles? Why can't they take *his* memory? Why does it have to be me?' said Freya, her frustration boiling over.

Charles exhaled deeply, steadying herself.

'Because you're the one who's accused him of rape. Plain and simple. They need your memory to compare to your testimony.'

Freya's voice dropped, bitter and laced with distrust. 'They're just trying to trip me up.'

Charles didn't argue. Instead, she closed the distance

between them and pulled Freya into another tight embrace. Her voice was a quiet promise as she held her close.

'We won't let that happen, Frey. I swear to you; we won't let that happen.'

▶❚❚

The hearing room was vast, imposing, and eerily empty. Sunlight filtered through partially drawn blinds, casting long, slatted shadows across the polished floor. The walls were lined with shelves of old legal tomes, their cracked and faded spines a stark contrast to the sleek, modern equipment set up in the centre of the room. A young video technician, barely in his twenties, hovered over the device, his hands moving too quickly as he adjusted dials and checked the screen. His nervous energy was palpable and put Freya on edge just watching him. Tugging at one of the blinds to darken the room, he gestured awkwardly towards a single chair positioned in front of the machine.

Charles led Freya to the chair, guiding her gently.

Freya sat down heavily, her expression guarded.

Charles held out a small cup. 'It's just water,' she said softly.

Freya took the cup, sipping slowly before setting it aside.

Charles pulled a chair close to her, her presence steady and reassuring. The video technician stood awkwardly nearby, wiping his hands on his trousers as though unsure what to do with himself.

'Alright,' Charles said, her voice low and calm. 'Let's do this.'

Freya reached out and placed her hand over Charles's, squeezing it tightly. Charles gave her a brief, firm squeeze in return before straightening up and stepping aside. She folded her arms and positioned herself in the corner, her eyes never leaving Freya.

The technician fumbled with the device, lifting a sleek silver headband dotted with glowing sensors. Freya tilted her head slightly, her face unreadable, and allowed him to fit the band snugly around her forehead.

'If you could close your eyes, it might help limit distractions,' he suggested.

Freya closed her eyes as the technician moved swiftly, plugging the headband into the MCD – the Memory Capture Device. The machine hummed to life, the screen flickering as it began to sync with the sensors.

'So,' the technician began, glancing at his clipboard. 'The incident took place on second of February, 2027, at around 11:00 PM. Is that correct?'

'Yes,' Freya replied quietly.

He set the clipboard aside and typed the date and time into the machine. Then, he crouched slightly to meet her gaze. Freya opened her eyes briefly, locking onto his, before closing them again.

'I'd like you to think about that day,' he continued. 'Perhaps an hour before the incident. Something you remember clearly.'

Freya nodded silently and the technician redirected

his attention to the screen. Slowly, the images began to materialise, fuzzy at first, then taking on a sickening clarity.

A room bathed in red light. The ceiling bulb flickered erratically, its harsh glare momentarily revealing the blurred outline of a man's face. The perspective lurched and swayed, the angles distorted and unsteady, like a half-formed memory.

'Do you have that in your mind?' the technician asked gently.

'I do,' Freya replied.

He adjusted the dial, freezing the visuals on the screen. The man's face came into focus now, captured in excruciating detail. Freya's stomach churned, a wave of nausea rising alongside a creeping shame. She turned her eyes away, but the image seemed to linger, burned into her mind. His face had reminded her that it was real.

'Now,' the technician continued, 'I'd like you to think about the last thing you remember, four or five hours after the incident. Focus on a moment, perhaps how you felt. Something that anchors you there.'

Freya hesitated, her breathing uneven. Finally, she spoke. 'I called my mum.'

'Perfect,' the technician replied with an encouraging nod. 'Do you remember the conversation?'

'Some of it,' Freya said. 'I was still slurring from the drugs.'

'Does anything stand out?'

'She asked me if I'd done something stupid. She sounded afraid,' said Freya, her gaze fixed on the screen.

The image of a phone ringing flickered to life, accompanied by a faint, distorted tone. The technician adjusted the dial, fast-forwarding the playback. Freya flinched slightly as the sound sharpened, her mother's voice breaking through the room like an echo, dragging the memories back into focus, sharper now, more distinct.

'Got it! You can open your eyes now,' the technician

said, relief colouring his voice.

But Freya had only briefly closed them. The technician moved to the blinds, tugging them open to let in a streak of light. Charles stepped forward, her presence grounding, and took Freya's hand in her own.

'We've got the memory,' the technician explained, adjusting a final setting on the machine. 'The machine is finishing the recollection process now. It won't take much longer. Feel free to drink your water.'

'Told you it wouldn't take long,' Charles said with a small smile. 'It's all done now. We're almost there.'

Freya frowned, her voice uncertain. 'Are you sure you've got it all? I don't feel like it's caught everything.'

The technician glanced up from his equipment, his tone calm but sure. 'We've captured about eight hours of recollection,' he said.

'Can I watch it?' Freya asked.

The technician hesitated, avoiding her gaze as he shook his head.

'At some point, you will,' Charles interjected. 'But not today. We'll need to submit a formal request for access after the court proceedings are finalised.'

'But it's my memory,' Freya said, frustration creeping into her voice.

'It is,' Charles acknowledged. 'But it's in the court's hands now. It will be transcribed and summarised for readability. You'll receive a copy.'

Freya's brow furrowed. 'You mean they might not even watch it?'

'They'll review the parts used as evidence,' she explained. 'The full extraction will be archived permanently.'

Freya nodded reluctantly, her shoulders sagging under the weight of the process and the fresh recollections that had been dragged, unwillingly, to the forefront of her mind. *At least this part is over*, she thought, clinging to the faint hope that she might finally begin to put it all behind her. She had done everything she could, every agonising step, and now it was no longer in her hands. His fate lay with the law, and she could only hope they would make the right decision.

▶ ||

The living room was dim, lit only by the flickering glow of the television. Freya sat curled on the sofa, knitting something soft and woollen, her focus shifting back and forth between the steady click of her needles and the news playing on the screen. Her phone buzzed on the cushion beside her, but she ignored it, her hands continuing their rhythmic motion. The caller ID flashed again. She let it ring out, her eyes fixed on the small, comforting loops of yarn.

Her attention wavered as the news anchor's voice sharpened into focus. Freya glanced up just as the screen cut to a story about abortion laws being debated in the courts. Footage of protesters filled the frame, their signs stark against a grey backdrop. The camera switched to the presenter, his tone matter-of-fact yet laden with hope.

'Abortion could once again be legalised in Wales,' he announced, *'as the country moves to split from the UK, challenging laws imposed two years ago. Mounting pressure from the Labour government suggests change may be imminent.'*

Freya sighed and reached into her basket for another ball of yarn, wincing as her finger caught on the exposed blade of a pair of scissors. Blood welled up, and she instinctively put the finger to her lips, sucking away the sting as the presenter continued in the background.

'Women are reportedly facing a major economic crisis and deteriorating mental health since the bill was passed during the third lockdown. Welsh women's group 'WAM' has been picketing against what they see as outdated, misogynistic values trampling on women's rights. Spokesperson Malida Rielly had this to say. . .'

Freya's phone buzzed again, breaking her concentration. This time, she grabbed it, pressing it to her ear. 'Sorry, Mum. I was in the shower.'

Her mother's voice came through, familiar and concerned. 'Not again, love.'

'No, not like that,' Freya said sharply, her tone cutting through the room before softening into something more fragile. 'Just. . . you know.'

Her mother hesitated on the other end of the line, the silence stretching out before it broke with a sigh. 'Charles called me today. She mentioned you're getting everything sorted for the trial. Do you need me to drive you, darling?'

Freya stood abruptly, abandoning her knitting on the sofa, the loose strands unravelling slightly. She paced the room, her movements restless, before heading into the kitchen. She opened a drawer, rummaging for plasters, her hands shaking as she found the box.

'There won't be a trial, Mum,' she said finally, pulling out a plaster and setting it on the counter. 'Didn't Matt tell you?' There was a pause, a hesitation so faint Freya almost didn't catch it.

Then, her mother's voice, soft and tentative. 'Oh, Frey. He mentioned Bryce's deal, I didn't realise. Why didn't you call? Or pick up your phone? I would have come with you.'

Freya's jaw tightened. She peeled the wrapper off the plaster with a quick, jerky motion and pressed it onto her finger.

'It took five minutes, Mum,' she said flatly, her voice devoid of emotion as if that would make it easier.

'Just five minutes?' her mother repeated, the disbelief cracking through her tone.

'Yeah,' Freya replied, her voice clipped. 'It was weird. Like they just uploaded my head to the Cloud.'

The silence that followed was heavier this time, laden with things neither of them wanted to say. Her mother broke it first, her voice softening to the point of almost breaking. 'Have you spoken to the therapist?'

Freya closed her eyes and exhaled sharply, pinching

the bridge of her nose.

'Mum, I don't need this right now. Please,' Her words were firm, but underneath they wavered slightly. 'I'm not okay, but I'm. . . okay. I just don't want to talk about it anymore. The verdict will be out within the next week or so. They'll show the extraction there, and then it'll all be over. I just want it to end.'

Her mother hesitated, clearly weighing her response, before changing the subject with deliberate gentleness. 'Are you coming to Emilia's birthday at the weekend? It might be good for you to get out. We all miss you terribly. The kids miss you. . .' she trailed off, the weight of her words settling in the quiet. 'It's been two months, Frey.'

Freya's hands trembled slightly as she smoothed the plaster over her finger. She stood at the counter for a moment, staring at the faint pattern of wood grain beneath her hands. When she finally spoke, her voice was softer, unsteady.

'I know how long it's been,' she said, almost to herself.

She swallowed hard before adding, 'I'll see how I feel.'

The line went quiet, her mother holding back words that Freya wasn't ready to hear.

'I can come by and pick you up,' her mother offered. 'Charles will be there.'

'Maybe. I just. . . I don't know. I'll let you know,' Freya's answer was quiet, uncertain. She felt the guilt creep in.

Her mother's voice softened. 'Okay, darling. Well, you know where I am. I'll give you a call tomorrow.'

'You don't have to keep calling, Mum,' Freya said softly.

'I want to,' her mother hesitated before replying. 'Goodnight, darling.'

'Night, Mum,' Freya whispered, ending the call.

She slumped back onto the sofa, her eyes drifting across the room until it came to a photograph on the mantelpiece, a picture of her with her children and Matt. The weight of it all bore down on her as she stared, silent and still. She had let this get the better of her. She would go to Emilia's birthday if it killed her. For them, she would go for them.

▶||

At three in the morning, Freya woke to the sound of running water, the steady rhythm slicing through the heavy silence of the house. Beneath it, faint and fractured, came another sound. A soft, broken whimpering; it was so quiet it could have been her imagination. But it wasn't. She knew it wasn't. A chill swept over her, and the hairs on her arms stood on end. She sat up abruptly, her breath catching in her throat, and swung her legs over the side of the bed. Her eyes flicked to the door, ajar, and the faint strip of light bled into the hallway beyond. Freya crossed the room in a few hesitant steps and paused in the doorway. Her heart was pounding, each beat reverberating in her ears. She stood there for a moment, staring at the sliver of light beneath the bathroom door, her pulse quickening.

She stepped into the hallway, her bare feet soundless on the cool wood. Her breath came shallow and fast as she moved closer, the faint whimpering mingling with the rhythmic patter of the water. Her hand trembled as she reached for the handle. She hesitated before she turned it.

The latch clicked softly in the silence, and the door creaked open. The bathroom was shrouded in thick, clinging steam, the mirror fogged over, its surface blurred and ghostly. The water continued to run, the sound echoing in the base of the bath, louder now, insistent. Freya's gaze was drawn to the shower, to the figure standing beneath the spray.

She froze, her breath catching in her throat. Her duplicate stood there, the same green dress clinging to her body – only now, its fabric had darkened, as if it had absorbed every terrible thing that had happened. The water streamed over her head, soaking her hair and plastering it to her face. Her head was bowed, shoulders trembling as the spray beat down on her. Broken sobs escaped her lips between ragged breaths.

Freya couldn't move. Her feet felt rooted to the floor, her mind caught between disbelief and rising dread. The steam swirled around her, the air thick with the scent of damp fabric and something metallic, something sharp. The figure in the shower didn't look up, didn't acknowledge her presence, but somehow Freya felt seen. The feeling wrapped around her chest was constricting, suffocating.

The sobbing grew louder, fraying at the edges, more distorted, like something breaking apart. Freya wanted to move, to back away, to run. But she couldn't. The weight of it, the memories stitched into that green dress were blackening as it grew darker, her reflection holding her captive.

'This isn't real,' Freya whispered, her voice shaky and small. The water continued to pour relentlessly, cascading over the dress. Freya took a single step back, her hand still on the doorframe. Her duplicate's shoulders jerked slightly, as if she'd heard. Freya froze, unable to tear her gaze away as the figure's head slowly lifted. The face that turned towards her was her own, but the eyes, those weren't hers. They were empty, hollow pits, black and endless, filled with anguish. The broken capillaries spread like black mold across her face until they reached her mouth, which opened wide and unnatural.

Her duplicate let out a guttural scream as blackness filled the air. Freya stumbled back, slipping on the wet tiles, the sound ripping through her like a jagged blade. She screamed too now, her voice mingling with the nightmarish banshee, until her own cry snapped her awake.

She bolted upright in her bed, gasping for air, her nightclothes damp with sweat. The room was dark, unnaturally so; the shadows were thick and impenetrable. Her eyes darted around, trying to anchor herself, to convince herself it had only been a dream.

And then she saw it in the corner of the room. Among

the darkest shadows, another figure loomed. Its outline was indistinct, more suggestion than substance, but Freya's stomach turned. She recognised that shape. She knew it, every fibre of her being screamed the same thing. It was *him*.

Her breath caught in her throat as she stared, paralysed. The figure didn't move, didn't speak, but its presence was suffocating, its malice palpable. The office hummed to life around her, phones ringing, printers buzzing, voices echoing through the walls. She'd been so eager, so sure she'd found *the* perfect job. But then Bryce appeared at her desk, leaning just a little too close. His stink wrapped around her, like a fog, she couldn't see past.

'You'll do well here,' he said, his voice quiet, smooth like silk. It would have sounded like encouragement to anyone else. But she knew better now. She had been chosen. As his sport, his prize. She had never been a colleague to him.

Her chest tightened, the sensation crawling up her

throat as she watched him edge closer into the darkness. Her trembling hand reached out for the lamp on her bedside table, but she dared not take her eyes off the silhouette, her fingers fumbling over the switch as she stared into the blackness.

With a sharp click, the light flooded the room. The corner was empty. Her heart pounded against her ribs as her eyes scoured every inch of her bedroom, desperate for any sign that he had been there, that she wasn't losing her mind. But there was nothing. Only the same corner, now harmless in the warm glow of the lamp.

Freya sat back, her breaths shallow and uneven, her body locked in a trembling tension as the echoes of the dream lingered. The figure's presence had felt so real, as if it had reached across the boundary of her subconscious to drag its fingers through her waking life. And as always, it left something behind – a weight that sunk down deep in her chest, a sickly knot of fear and self-loathing that twisted like a knife.

She recognised the feeling. It was familiar now, though no less terrifying. Each time it returned, it burrowed deeper, like a parasite feeding on the darkest corners of her mind, leaving her hollow and raw. Then would come the voice, haunting and persistent. It whispered to her from the shadows, coiling her thoughts like smoke, winding around the fragile parts of her. It didn't demand. It simply offered a suggestion, calm and insidious: *You can make it stop. You know how.*

Freya's hands tightened around the blanket, her nails digging into the fabric. In the quiet hours of the night, when the world was still and her defences were at their weakest, she had thought about it. About ending it. About how it might be better – easier for everyone. Her family didn't deserve the fragile mess she had become. She could picture their lives without her, untangled from the burden of her brokenness. The thought crept in uninvited, twisting her love into something warped and unrecognisable, convincing her that their lives would be easier without the broken mess of a mother, of a wife.

But why? Why would she give him that? Why would she allow him to take everything, not just her body, her safety, her peace of mind, but her very self? He had already stolen so much, ripped her life apart. Freya closed her eyes tightly, forcing the tears back as her nails dug into the blanket beneath her. Her breath steadied as she forced the darkness back into its corner. The fear, the self-loathing, the doubt – they would all return as they always did. But so would this fire, this tiny ember of defiance smouldering inside her.

He had taken so much from her. But he would not take everything. She would not go down without a fight.

▶︎❚❚

Freya stood in her bedroom, pulling outfit after outfit from the wardrobe, each one discarded into a growing pile on the bed. Nothing felt right. Nothing fit, not the way she wanted it to. Finally, she settled on a fitted black dress, tugging a soft cardigan over the top in a futile attempt to disguise the subtle curve she knew was there, the shape of something she wasn't ready to face.

She turned to the mirror, her brow furrowed in dissatisfaction as her fingers hovered near her stomach, straightening the fabric. She tied her hair up tightly, only to pull it loose moments later, dissatisfied with both choices. Slipping on her shoes, she straightened her cardigan, fidgeting with the hem before turning back to the mirror for one last look. Her expression was empty, her gaze distant, as though she barely recognised the person staring back at her. With a small sigh, she turned away and closed the door.

Freya stood at the bus stop, her arms wrapped around a bottle of prosecco in a wine bag and a *Peppa Pig* birthday bag. Her gaze drifted, unfocused, until a woman with a pram approached and sat nearby. Freya smiled softly at the little girl in the pram, who stared back shyly.

'She loves Peppa Pig,' the mother offered with a smile.

'So do mine,' Freya said, leaning slightly towards the child. 'Who's your favourite?'

The little girl didn't respond, her gaze fixed firmly on the ground.

'She's shy,' the mother said with a chuckle. 'But she loves Grandpa Pig.'

'Oh, he's my favourite too,' Freya said, forcing a small laugh.

The woman glanced at Freya, hesitating before speaking again. 'How long do you have?'

Freya blinked, confused. 'Huh?'.

The woman's expression shifted awkwardly as she realised her mistake. 'Oh, I'm sorry. You're not pregnant, are you? I've just gone and ruined your day.'

Freya managed to force a strained smile, her chest tightening as she forced herself to respond. 'It's okay. I am. . . I just didn't think I was showing too much yet. I'm only just over two months.'

The woman's cheeks flushed with embarrassment.

She looked as though she might say something else, but instead, she turned her attention back to her child. As the bus pulled into the stop, she gestured for Freya to board first.

'Oh, I'm waiting for the next one,' Freya said quietly. The woman nodded and stepped onto the bus. Freya watched it pull away before turning and walking in the opposite direction, her breath coming in shallow gasps as she fought back tears.

Freya slammed the front door behind her, the sound reverberating through the empty house like a gunshot. The walls shuddered under the force, as though the house itself had felt her anger. She stalked into the kitchen, yanking the bottle of prosecco from the garish gift bag, and twisted it open with a sharp, decisive motion. The pop of the cork felt loud in the silence. She grabbed the nearest mug, a chipped ceramic one with a faded unicorn that her daughter Aeda always pined for, and poured the liquid until it was full. She turned and caught sight of herself in the mirror that hung crookedly on the far wall. Her glare cut through the reflection like a blade. Her eyes, rimmed red with exhaustion and frustration, dropped to her stomach. Her dress clung there, seemingly rounder than she remembered, almost mocking her. The anger surged, hot and immediate, a fire roaring to life in her chest.

Freya walked into the bathroom and turned on the shower. The water blasted against the tiles, the sound deafening but calming. She stepped in fully clothed, the mug still in her hand, the prosecco sloshing onto the bathroom floor. The hot water hit her skin, soaking her hair and dress in uneven streams that plastered the fabric to her body. She stood motionless for a while under the spray, her breath coming out in ragged bursts, but she didn't sob like she had so many times in the last month. Instead, she felt another surge of anger in her stomach.

When she emerged, her mascara was smudged and blotchy beneath her eyes. Wrapping herself in a towel, she poured another mug of prosecco before tipping it into the sink, the sharp smell of the alcohol rising as it swirled down the drain. Freya stumbled to the sofa, still damp. She sank into the cushions, her body heavy, her mind buzzing. The house was silent now, the kind of oppressive silence that comes when an event takes all life from it, it pressed down on her like a weight. Eventually, she fell into a restless sleep, her dreams fractured and jagged like shards of glass.

She awoke to the sound of running water and soft, low sobbing. Sitting upright, she listened intently as a strange, morose hum filled the silence and seemed to crawl up her spine. Freya's eyes darted around the darkened room, her mind struggling to catch up. Rising slowly, she followed the sound, barefoot against the cold floor. The hum grew louder as she ascended the stairs, the wood creaking softly beneath her weight. At the top, she saw a faint sliver of light escaping from beneath the bathroom door. She took another step, her feet pausing when she noticed the footprints. Freya's hand trembled as she reached for the handle. Slowly, she pushed the door open, the latch clicking softly as steam billowed out and curled around her like grasping fingers.

The bathroom mirror was fogged, but the figure inside the shower was unmistakable. Freya knew her now, she'd been following her into dreams, waiting for her to fall asleep. Her breath hitched as she took a step closer.

Freya's double stood fully clothed beneath the spray, the same green dress clinging to her body. She cradled her abdomen as blood pooled at her feet from dark, viscous streams between her legs, which swirled toward the drain. Her face was twisted in anguish, her mouth opening and closing in a soundless scream. Freya's stomach turned, but she couldn't look away. Her reflection cried out, the sound raw and guttural, her head jerked up. The eyes, her eyes, snapped open and locked onto Freya's own; they were filled with something dark and unreadable.

A gasp tore from Freya's throat as she stumbled

backwards, her legs giving way. She hit the doorframe hard, her chest heaving, the air forced out of her lungs. With her back against the hallway wall, she tried to steady herself as her chest tightened.

The sound of the water stopped abruptly, just a faint stream of light spilled out from beneath the door. Freya stood there, trembling. Her fingers hovered over the handle but she couldn't bring herself to open it. She sank to her knees and leaned down, peering beneath the door. At first, she saw nothing, just shadows and light from passing cars. But then, something moved. A pair of eyes locked onto hers, unblinking and unfeeling. This time, they were *his*.

Freya sat upright on the sofa, her body drenched in sweat, her heart hammering as the memory of his eyes bore into her. Her breaths rose into deep gasps, her hands clutching the blanket draped across her lap. The room seemed to shift and sway until it steadied, the faint glow of a streetlamp spilling through the curtains, bringing her back to the room. Her eyes darted around until they landed on the figure in the doorway.

She jumped, startled, until she realised it was Charles. Her face was concerned, her expression unreadable as she took a tentative step forward.

'Freya?' she said softly.

Freya didn't answer. She stared at her friend, her pulse still hammering as the memory of the dream lingered.

'Still having those nightmares?' Charles asked.

Freya didn't look up right away. Her fingers idly brushed over the fabric of her dressing gown, finding a loose thread. When she finally spoke, her voice was flat, stripped bare.

'They never left. But this one was different. . .'

Her hands moved instinctively to cradle her stomach, as though protecting something she wasn't sure she wanted.

'I was miscarrying,' she said, her words hollow, like they belonged to someone else. She didn't cry. The tears had come and gone, leaving her numb.

'It's still possible, Frey,' Charles said quietly. 'There are places. Scotland, even. Quiet clinics in Edinburgh. Most of us turn a blind eye to it if it's done properly. You could. . . you know,' Her voice was laced with a quiet encouragement, her words hanging in the air like a lifeline.

But Freya shook her head, her shoulders stiffening.

Her voice, when it came, was barely above a whisper. 'It's not her fault,' she paused, the words tasting bitter in her mouth.

'I just... I need to know if it's *his* first. Matt and I have been trying for so long,' her fingers tightened around her stomach. The weight of the words pressed against her chest, and for a moment, it felt like she couldn't breathe.

Charles hesitated. 'It's a girl?' she asked softly. 'How do you know?'

Freya's gaze flicked toward her, a faint glimmer of something passing through her eyes.

'I just know,' she said. Her words were steady now, though they certainly felt like both a comfort and a curse.

Slowly, she rose from the sofa, brushing her hands down her sides, as though trying to physically shake off the weight pressing her down. She moved to tidy the room, a quiet compulsion to bring order to the chaos she couldn't control. She picked up stray items and placed them into boxes. Her movements were methodical and her mind was elsewhere. When her fingers brushed over Charles's gun holster, she hesitated, the cold metal grounding her for a moment. She held it too long, her fingertips tracing the edges of the weapon, and thoughts she didn't dare let solidify flickered through her mind.

Charles stepped forward, calm but deliberate, and gently took the holster from Freya's hands. She didn't say anything, just reattached it to her side and bent down to help with the tidying. When they were done, Freya carried the boxes out to the wheelie bins.

The cold air bit at her cheeks as Charles held the bin lids open for Freya to tip the contents inside. When the last box was emptied, Charles broke the silence.

'I hope you don't mind me popping in like this,' she said softly. 'Your mum was worried when you didn't show.'

Freya shook her head faintly, the corners of her mouth twitching into something that might have been a smile but never quite got there.

'No problem,' she said, her voice measured, though exhaustion seeped through her words. 'I think I'll feel better after next week, when it's all done.'

'Hopefully, he'll get what's coming to him,' Charles said, her tone sharp and venomous as her hand moved to her holster.

Freya didn't respond right away. Her hands gripped the edges of the empty box, her knuckles white against the plastic. Her expression grew distant until her eyes fixed on some unseen point.

'I mean, I'll know,' she said finally, her voice quiet. 'If she's Matt's, we can move on. And if not. . .' she trailed off, the weight of her unspoken thoughts weighing on her. 'At least I'll know,' she finished.

The decision loomed over her like a shadow, dark and inevitable. If the baby wasn't Matt's. . . She didn't let herself finish the thought. She'd made peace with the idea that he might get off, that the verdict might not swing her way. She knew the system wasn't built to help people like her. But this was different. If the baby was *his*. . . Her mind wandered to the possibilities, the grim realities.

She'd thought about it before, in the quiet moments when the world felt too heavy. Scotland. Edinburgh. A quiet clinic where no one would know her name. She could disappear for a few days, arrange everything without fuss, without questions. She could come back to a world that didn't feel like it was suffocating her. But now, as the DNA test and the verdict loomed closer, the clarity she thought she'd found was slipping through her fingers, leaving behind nothing but the mess of it all.

She sighed deeply, gripping the box as though it might somehow steady her. Charles's presence beside her was a small comfort, but nothing could quiet the storm brewing. Not yet.

The two women embraced tightly before Charles climbed into her car. Freya waved her off from the drive, standing still as the car disappeared from view. For a long moment, she stayed there, the cold night air biting at her skin. The weight of the decision pressing against her chest. She had to know. Even if the answer might tear her apart.

▶ll

Freya sat in the waiting room, staring at the crass laminated poster on the wall. *DNA Testing: Answers When You Need Them Most.* The words were printed in bold blue letters, like they were advertising something as simple as a flu jab or travel inoculations.

Her hands twisted in her lap and her knee shook

nervously. The air in the clinic smelled faintly of antiseptic and coffee. The walls were a soft, neutral beige – designed, she supposed, to be calming. But nothing about this moment felt calm.

She checked the time on her phone. Five minutes past their appointment. Still no call from Matt. Had she been expecting too much? The thought had been gnawing at her all morning.

Matt had said he'd be here. He'd promised. But what if he changed his mind? What if the weight of all this, the appointment, the truth they were about to uncover, became too much? She took a slow breath, exhaling through her nose, trying to steady herself.

The receptionist tapped at a keyboard, her nails clicking against the keys. Behind her, a woman spoke softly into a phone, nodding as though the person on the other end could see her.

Freya had spent months imagining this baby. A little girl. She and Matt had talked about names, dreamt of the future, of who she might be. But then *he* had happened, and suddenly, all of it, the hope, the excitement, the certainty, had shattered into something unrecognisable. And now, this test. The one that would tell her if the baby was Matt's or *his* made her want to vomit.

The nausea wasn't just morning sickness. It was fear, coiled tight inside her, in the pit of her stomach, making it hard to swallow. She'd been living in limbo, trapped between two futures, waiting for the moment that would decide which one was hers, when the door opened and Matt walked in. Relief enveloped her, which was quickly replaced by dread.

He looked around, his eyes scanning the room until they landed on her. He exhaled, gave her a small, tight smile and crossed the floor in a few long strides. Without a word, he sat beside her, his hands already reaching for hers. She let him take them and he squeezed gently.

'I'm here,' he said.

Freya nodded, swallowing past the lump in her throat.

'I thought maybe. . .'

'I know,' he said, as if reading the rest of her sentence before she could say it. *I thought maybe you wouldn't come. I thought maybe you'd had enough.*

He turned her hands over in his, brushing his thumb lightly against her palm. 'No matter what this says, Frey, we'll figure it out. Okay? We'll be okay.'

Her breath shuddered, and she forced herself to nod. She wanted to believe him.

'Even if it's—'

'Even if,' Matt interrupted softly. 'Whatever you decide, I'll be here.'

The words settled over her like a blanket, warm and reassuring, even as the fear still twisted inside her. Matt handed her a paper cup of tea he'd been holding onto.

'I don't want to rush you,' he said. 'The children and I can stay at Mum's as long as you need. But if you're ready for us, for me to come home, if you think that's something you'd want, I'm here.'

Before Freya could reply, a nurse appeared in the doorway, clipboard in hand. 'Freya Sloane?'

Freya stood, her legs unsteady beneath her, but Matt's grip on her hand didn't loosen. He stood with her, walked beside her, and when she hesitated at the door, he squeezed her hand again.

'I'm right here,' he murmured.

The nurse's face was unreadable. She held the folder close to her chest, and Freya thought she might be sick.

Matt sat beside her in a blue plastic chair that reminded her of school. He took her hand, grounding her, steadying her. But even with his warmth, she felt cold. The room had shrunk to just this moment.

The nurse cleared her throat. 'We have the results,' she said, flipping open the folder.

Freya held her breath, bracing for the impact. *Say it. Just say it.*

'The test confirms that the baby's father is Matthew Sloane.'

Freya blinked. The words didn't sink in; her brain had been expecting the worst and couldn't quite process them.

'Matt. . .' Her voice cracked. She turned to him, her vision blurring with unshed tears.

Matt let out a breath, one he'd been holding in since she had revealed her pregnancy. His grip on her hand tightened and she was suddenly in his arms. He pulled her close, pressing his face against her hair.

'It's ours, Frey,' he whispered.

'She's ours,' said Freya under her breath. The relief had hit her all at once. The weight of the last four weeks, when she had told him, finally lifted. The fear, the uncertainty, the quiet, gnawing horror of what could have been were all gone.

And in its place, something else. Anger. Her stomach clenched as the relief burned away, replaced by something hotter, sharper, fiercer. He had taken so much from her. Stolen her safety, shattered her peace of mind, and made her doubt everything, including herself. And he could have taken *this*. Her daughter. The one she and Matt had dreamed about, prayed for. He could have made her question the one thing that had been hers from the very start.

Her fingers curled into fists and Matt gripped her tighter. Freya had been living in fear for too long, waiting for justice, waiting for other people to decide what happened next. The trial loomed, and she had spent so long dreading it, wondering if the court would believe her. But right now, she didn't care what they thought. She knew the truth. And she would make sure that one way or another, he would never take anything from her again.

She looked up at Matt, her chest still rising and falling too fast, her pulse hammering in her ears.

He cupped her face, his thumbs brushing away tears she hadn't even realised had fallen.

'It's over,' he murmured.

Freya swallowed hard.

'Not yet,' she said, her voice steady. 'But soon.'

▶❙❙

Morning came slow, its oppressive grey sky anchoring Freya to her bed. Lying still, she stared at the ceiling and listened to the slow tick of the clock on the wall. Each passing second brought her closer to the verdict, perhaps closer to *him*.

Freya hadn't slept. She hadn't even tried. What was the point? Sleep wouldn't change the outcome. It wouldn't alter the way the jury might look at her, at him, at the story. They would fabricate or pick apart, like scavengers stripping the meat from her bones. Would they believe her? Would they see her for what she was – a victim? Or a woman who had regrets. A woman who had made a mistake. A woman who was lying to save her marriage. She swallowed against the rising nausea in her throat and turned onto her side, eyes drifting to the empty space where Matt should have been. He was downstairs. He hadn't slept much either. The weight of the upcoming day sat between them like a barrier neither of them could cross. *If the jury doesn't believe me, will he?*

The thought made her stomach twist violently, and she pressed a hand to it, as if she could physically push the fear away. She and Matt had been trying for a little girl. Talking about names, picking out colours for a nursery they hadn't even started decorating. She'd imagined their daughter a hundred times, maybe a thousand, Matt's eyes, her nose. But then *he* had happened. And now, even after she knew, after the result that should have brought relief, there was still doubt. A doubt that crept in during the silent moments, in the way Matt's hands hesitated before resting on her stomach, in the way his smile didn't quite reach his eyes when he spoke about the future. If the verdict was negative, would Matt pull away? Would she wake up one day and find him gone?

The house was too quiet. No creaking of the floorboards from the hallway, no sound of little Aeda and

Charlie running up and down the hall or Matt making coffee, no hum of the television playing the morning news. Just silence. Freya forced herself upright, the weight of her body feeling too much. She sat at the edge of the bed, rubbing a hand down her face before pressing her fingers into her temples. The nausea hadn't eased. Her limbs felt heavy and tight, as if she were already bracing for impact. She didn't want to go. She wanted to stay here, cocooned in the stale safety of her bedroom. If she didn't, then there would be no justice. No closure. No end to any of this. And if *he* walked, if they let him go, what then? Would she ever feel safe again?

She dressed slowly, each movement mechanical. She caught a glimpse of herself in the mirror as she pulled her hair back, and for a moment, she recognised the woman staring back. A woman waiting to be told whether her pain was real. Whether it mattered to her anymore. She stepped into the hallway and found Matt at the bottom of the stairs, a mug of coffee held loosely in his hand.

He looked up at her, his eyes tired, his face unreadable.

'You ready?' he asked.

She opened her mouth, but nothing came out. *No. I'm not ready. I will never be ready.* But that didn't matter, it was here, whether she was ready or not.

▶️⏸️

The courtroom smelled like old wood and dust, like something preserved in time, a place where justice was supposed to be weighed, measured and served. But Freya had known from the beginning, long before today, long before she made her statement and had her extraction, that justice wasn't a guarantee. She sat at the front as they read out his sentence, willing *him* to look at her. Her fingers dug into her palms, nails pressing so deep they left half-moons in her skin. Matt was beside her, his hand a solid weight against her back she held her hand to her stomach feeling the small little person inside her. The jury had come back quickly. Too quickly and before getting here she had wondered what this had meant.

Her attacker sat across from her, his lawyer whispering in his ear. *He* looked calm. Relaxed. Like this was a meeting he'd already planned for. Freya thought about the way he had built his reputation; the same way men like him always did. The kind that took up too much space in meetings, laughed too loud in offices that weren't theirs and spoke in jokes that weren't really jokes. The ones who turned workplaces into boys' clubs, where power was a game and women were the sport. The thought made her stomach churn. And then there was that smirk. The same one he'd worn when he flirted with her, when he made her uncomfortable at work. When she laughed off his inappropriate comments, forced to pretend that it didn't make her skin crawl. The same smirk he had on now, as if this whole thing had been a minor inconvenience.

The judge cleared his throat.

'In the matter of *The Crown versus Bryce Thompson*, the jury has found the defendant guilty on all charges.'

For half a second, Freya thought she might be sick. The air in the courtroom seemed to shift, her ears ringing as the words landed.

Guilty.

She barely had time to process it before the judge continued.

'Given the defendant's cooperation in assisting law enforcement with identifying other individuals engaged in sexual misconduct within the workplace, along with his exemplary behaviour during custody and the time he has already served, the court has determined that a further term of eighteen months imprisonment is appropriate.'

Freya's breath hitched.

Less than two years. Not enough. Not nearly enough.

She had imagined this moment over and over, had lain awake at night, dreading the possibility that he might walk free. But in her worst nightmares, she had never prepared herself for this feeling. Of justice measured and lukewarm. Of what felt more like a concession than a punishment. Her body was stiff, her hands clenched so tightly they ached. She wanted to scream. To stand up and ask the judge if he had any idea what this man had done to her, what he had stolen from her. If he knew what it was like to be afraid to walk alone, to sleep without waking in terror, to question every look, every touch, every moment of safety that had once felt like a given.

Fifteen months, maybe less, and then he'd be back. Back in the world, walking the streets, going to work, back with the boys, laughing.

Living!

Freya forced herself to look at him. *He* turned slightly, just enough to catch her eye. He wasn't smiling, not quite. But there was something there. A flicker of triumph. A look that told her he'd already started counting the days.

Her nails dug deeper into her palms. She felt Matt beside her, his presence solid and unmoving. He had promised that no matter what, they would be okay. But Freya wasn't sure what 'okay' even meant anymore.

No matter what the court had said, she knew the truth. Bryce Thompson wasn't done. She wouldn't be his last victim.

Eighteen months or less. That was how long she had to wait before he was free again. And then what? She didn't know. But as she watched them lead him out of the courtroom, his hands cuffed and his chin still held high, she realised one thing with absolute certainty: she would not spend that time waiting for him to walk free. The courthouse doors loomed ahead, and she pushed through them, stepping out into the cold afternoon air. The sky was dull, overcast, the kind of grey that swallowed light. It felt fitting. She didn't feel the cold. Didn't feel anything but the slow, creeping certainty settling deep inside her bones.

If the system wouldn't make him pay, *she* would.

She turned her head slightly, glancing over her shoulder just as Bryce Thomson walked through the doors. A smile twitched at the corner of his mouth, barely there, but she caught it. His flicker of triumph. Victory shone from his eyes and his smug face filled her with rage. Inside her, something snapped.

The rage that had burned so quietly for the last three months, slow, smouldering, contained, now erupted like molten lava, searing, carving through the last remaining pieces of her restraint. She had been waiting for the justice that would never come. Now, she would wait no longer. Freya stepped forward, her mind made up. One way or another, she was going to make damn sure Bryce Thomson would never hurt anyone ever again.

▶ll

Freya walked slowly along the edge of the lake, the crunch of gravel beneath her feet barely audible over the soft rustle of the breeze. She paused, her eyes fixed on the rippling water, its gentle movement offering a fleeting moment of peace amidst the storm inside. In the clearing behind her, Charles appeared. She walked towards her with the same deliberation, as though trying to delay the conversation that was to come.

'Charles,' Freya said softly, her voice carrying the weight of fatigue.

'I know what you're going to say,' Charles replied, her tone tinged with a bittersweet understanding.

Freya exhaled slowly, her gaze locked on the lake. 'I'm okay. Really, I am. I knew this was going to happen sooner or later. I don't want to say I told you so.'

Charles didn't respond immediately but nodded in acknowledgement, reaching out to take Freya's hand. Her grip was firm, grounding.

'I'm so sorry,' she said, apologising for the news she was about to repeat, though they both knew Freya had already heard it.

'I know,' Freya whispered, her lips pressed into a thin line.

'They released him earlier, for good behaviour,' Charles said hesitantly, as if weighing her words.

'I heard,' Freya said, her voice steady but hollow. Still,

her stomach sank just as it had the first time she'd heard the news. 'I just want to sort my life out. Try to figure out what's next.'

'We will get him, Frey,' Charles said, with quiet conviction. 'Two women have already come forward. You know that's because of you.'

Freya's expression remained unmoved.

'It doesn't help me sleep any better,' she said plainly.

Charles sighed, the breath heavy with frustration and helplessness. 'I know. But for now. . . what else can we do?'

Freya's gaze drifted downward, landing on the gun holster at Charles's side. Charles noticed but said nothing, letting the moment pass unspoken.

Breaking the silence, Freya spoke, her voice softer.

'Matt and I are giving things another try. We talked, and I've spoken to Aeda and Charlie about their baby sister. They're excited. We're going to try to make it work.'

Charles's features softened, her lips curving into a small smile. 'That's amazing, Frey. It's a big step. A good step. Back to some kind of normality.'

Freya nodded slowly, though she could feel the pull of anger lingering, tugging her thoughts backwards.

'I've just got a few things I need to do before we can move on from this, you know.'

Charles stepped closer, pulling Freya into a tight hug. Her voice, though steady, was laced with an edge of determination.

'*We* have something we need to do, Frey. I promised, didn't I? One way or another. He won't get to walk away from this.'

As Charles pulled back, Freya met her gaze, her own eyes shimmering with a mix of gratitude and pain. Freya felt an unspoken understanding in Charles's expression, a quiet and threatening promise. She didn't need to ask what Charles meant, she could feel it, a visceral certainty forged in shared rage and loyalty. Charles would find a way to make him pay, no matter what the law failed to do. Freya lifted a hand and rested it gently on Charles's face, her touch soft and full of unspoken words. She leaned forward, kissing each cheek of the woman she trusted completely in a gesture of thanks and recognition. The two women stood there, their silence heavy with understanding, a moment stretching between them like a vow. Charles nodded at Freya, who mirrored the gesture before stepping forward to embrace her friend once more, holding on tightly. This time, it wasn't just for comfort, it was for strength and the unshakable belief that Charles would do whatever was necessary to make him answer for what he had done.

▶ll

Bryce Thompson pulled into his driveway, his laughter rising over the hum of his engine. He had the easy, careless air of someone who believed he had no trouble in the world. The phone was pressed to his ear, his conversation light-hearted, punctuated with bursts of chuckles as he climbed out of the car and said his goodbyes. With the casual grace of routine, he popped the boot and began unloading shopping bags. A carton of eggs here, a loaf of bread there, each movement exuding the smug confidence of a man who thought he'd walked away unscathed, untouchable. But *they* had been watching.

For weeks, they had followed him. Unseen. Patient. Meticulous. Every step was calculated, the risk weighed up and re-evaluated with each passing day. Charles had mapped out the potential obstacles, spending night after night staking out the place. She had studied every inch of Bryce's property, the angles of the cameras, the blind spots where they could slip past unnoticed. She knew when the lights flicked on in the living room when Bryce would have his back turned, and which side of the field behind the house offered the easiest approach.

Freya had joined her when she could, moving through the field like a shadow, vanishing as if she'd never been there. No missteps. No mistakes. Bryce wouldn't see them coming.

They had waited for the right night, biding their time as they watched him settle back into his routine, as if prison had never touched him. After his early release, they saw the arrogance return, piece by piece as he brought home girls who giggled at the threshold before disappearing inside. In the mornings they had witnessed their walk of shame as he had sauntered back into his house, parading like a man who had beaten the system, who didn't even bother to throw a cursory glance over his shoulder.

He thought he was safe, untouchable. And they let him believe it – just like Freya had believed it before he assaulted her. She needed him leached from her life, to sever the cord completely. Bryce had to be stopped. Her child would not be born while he still clung to her.

Bryce had been released before the baby was even six months along, and Freya couldn't rest with him out there, living his life as though he had earned it. Every day Bryce existed, a part of her stayed trapped in that room, replaying what he had taken from her. She had wanted to draw a line in the sand and step over it. She wanted the past buried so deeply, that death seemed the only option. *It was him or her – and it couldn't be her.* After weeks of waiting, of pretending to live with the rage, the moment had finally arrived.

The door clicked shut behind him as he stepped into his house, sealing him inside the one place he believed he was safest. In the kitchen, he moved unhurriedly, his motions casual, as though life itself owed him its ease. The fridge door squeaked faintly as he slid the milk onto a shelf. He flicked the kettle on, and its low hiss began to fill the silence, growing steadily louder as it edged toward a boil.

He didn't notice her at first. Charles stood in the shadows of the doorway, dressed head to toe in a forensic suit. Her feet were wrapped in blue shoe covers that crinkled faintly with every step, though now she was motionless, watching. Her stillness was unnerving, her gaze locked onto him with a predator's focus. Every detail, every movement of his, she tracked with a quiet intensity. Her aim was steady, the barrel of her gun pointed at his head, the safety already off. She wasn't in a rush. She was waiting. Waiting for him to turn, to see her, to understand. To beg. Charles remained frozen in place, her focus unwavering.

The kettle hissed in a crescendo. The moment stretched, tense and unbearable, until his movements slowed. He turned, the laughter still faintly lingering on his face, only for it to drain away entirely when his eyes met hers. The look in her gaze left no room for doubt: his safety, his arrogance, his untouchable world had shattered. He froze the carton slack in his hand, his face blanching as the colour drained from it. The kettle's hiss turned into a shrill whistle, a morose undertone building beneath it like a heartbeat.

'But. . . you're an officer,' he stammered, his voice

barely audible over the noise.

Charles's face was impassive, her voice cutting through the rising din. 'And you're a rapist.'

Her gaze flicked to the side, and Freya stepped into the kitchen, clad in matching forensic gear. The suit stretched taut over her swollen stomach, now unmistakable at eight months. Her movements were slow and deliberate, her expression void of hesitation: she was there to end this. She didn't speak. She didn't need to.

Charles holstered her gun with measured calm, stepping behind Freya and placing her hands gently on her friend's arms, steadying her, grounding her.

Freya raised her weapon, her hands trembling faintly, but her resolve remained firm, etched into every line of her face.

The man's eyes darted to her stomach, widening with sudden, terrible clarity. His mouth opened, his lips moved wordlessly, but no sound came out.

He knew exactly what this was. Exactly why they

were here. His eyes drew down to her stomach again.

'Is it. . .' he began, his voice faltering into silence.

'No!' Freya spat, her tone sharp and unyielding.

'Please,' he begged, his voice trembling now, desperation bleeding through his words. 'Please, I'll go back, I'll tell them what I did. I'm so sorry,' he pleaded, his voice cracking. 'I was drunk, off my face. I would never have. . .'

Before he could say another word, Freya and Charles squeezed the trigger in unison. The gunshot exploded through the air, in a muffled punctuation to the kettle's relentless scream. Bryce staggered backwards as the bullet hit him square in the chest, a spray of red splattering across the pristine white cabinets behind him. The milk carton slipped from his grip, crashing to the floor, its contents spilling out and mingling with the blood pooling on the cold tiles. He collapsed in a heap gurgling as his body crumpled awkwardly, lifeless.

The kitchen fell into silence. The low, morose hum

that had underscored the moment softened, the kettle finally calming as the whistle subsided. The room, so full of tension moments ago, now felt eerily tranquil as dusk arrived and the last of the sunlight filtered out of the room.

Freya and Charles stood for a moment, motionless, framed against the chaos. Blood, milk and shattered glass lay strewn around them. Neither spoke. There was no need to. They simply turned and walked out, their movements deliberate, their footsteps careful but unhurried.

The door clicked shut behind them, sealing their vengeance. Outside, the two women crossed the field and slipped into the woods, the dark expanse of the canopy swallowing them as they moved towards a waiting car. Together, they climbed in, the weight of their actions settling over them. In the silence, Freya and Charles sat close, holding one another in a quiet embrace, their breaths steady but laden with the gravity of what they had done.

Matt glanced into the rear-view mirror; his expression

was unreadable as his eyes met Freya's. She nodded at him, subtly but resolute. Matt returned the nod, starting the engine without a word. The car rolled forward, the crunch of gravel beneath the tyres fading as the road stretched out before them.

Freya sank back into her seat, her eyes fixed on the rear window as the house, the blood and the chaos they'd left behind disappeared into the distance. *It's finally over*, she thought, her chest rising and falling with a newfound sense of finality. As the road behind them vanished into the darkness, Freya fixed her gaze on the horizon ahead, the lights blurred into a path that held a promise of something she hadn't felt in a long time, peace.

ACKNOWLEDGEMENTS

You meet a lot of people at university, and during my Master's in Filmmaking at Kingston School of Art, it was no different. What was different, however, were the mentors who truly inspired me. As a photographer eager to tell stories through different mediums, they provided me with the tools, guidance, and encouragement to do just that.

I will always be grateful to have been taught by Mick Kennedy. His influence shaped my creative journey in ways I will always cherish. Nelson Douglas, who continues to be my mentor and PhD supervisor at Kingston School of Art, his work continues to inspire me, and he remains a guiding force.

My deepest gratitude goes to Abbe Fletcher, who has generously shared her wisdom and time with me for the past six years – as a supervisor, a mentor, and a friend. Her unwavering support has made this book possible, and I am incredibly thankful for the feedback, encouragement, and belief she has given me. This journey has been all the better for it.

I would also like to extend my heartfelt thanks to the incredible team who helped bring this book to life. To my editors Miya and Alessandra, whose keen eyes and expertise refined my words and shaped this story into its final form. To my cover artist, Sophie for capturing the essence of this book so beautifully. To the typesetter Nick, for ensuring every page was just as it should be. And finally to my project editor Raphaela, whose guidance and organisation kept everything moving forward. Your dedication, skill, and hard work have made this book what it is, and I am truly grateful for every one of you.

I am also endlessly appreciative to everyone who has featured in my documentaries and photography over the years. Trusting someone to tell your story is no small feat, and I am truly honoured that you shared your time with me and allowed me into your life. It is because of you that I have these stories to tell.

I am incredibly grateful to my partner Chris, who has supported me throughout the duration of my PhD and the writing of this book – not just with words of encouragement, but with countless cups of tea and coffee, and the endless cycles of washing and cleaning while I've been lost in my work. To my cats – Jake and Elwood – who have been my ever-present writing companions, curling up beside me as I work.

Finally, I am grateful to my family – my foundation and my steadfast supporters. My mother, Susie, a firecracker of a woman, and my father, Mark, a natural storyteller who encouraged my love of books from a young age. My sister, Lottie, fierce, fabulous, and always just a phone call away, and my brother, Dan, who keeps me grounded with his sharp wit. My brother, George, a walking encyclopaedia, always ready with an answer for any question. And to my little Rose, whose kindness and encouragement remind me to keep going, even on the hardest days.

I couldn't have done this without all of you.

ABOUT THE AUTHOR

Louise Sands is a literary science fiction author from North London, whose work explores the intersection of dystopian futures and harsh contemporary realities. Growing up on a council estate in the 90s she developed an early fascination with dystopian science fiction – stories that mirrored the systemic struggles she saw around her.

Her writing is deeply influenced by her work as a documentary filmmaker and photographer, where she uncovers the unsettling truths of modern society. These experiences shape the dystopian landscapes of her fiction, blending speculative storytelling with themes of control, resistance, and survival.

Tonie is currently undertaking a PhD at Kingston School of Art, funded by Techne, with a research focus on the feminine condition, dystopia, and science fiction. Her screenplays and prose are born from the stark realities she has documented, transforming lived experiences into narratives that challenge, provoke, and unsettle.

ABOUT KUP

Kingston University Press has been publishing high-quality commercial and academic titles for over ten years. Our list has always reflected the diverse nature of the student and academic bodies at the university in ways that are designed to impact on debate, to hear new voices, to generate mutual understanding and to complement the values to which the university is committed.

Increasingly the books we publish are produced by students on the Kingston School of Art MA courses, often working with partner organisations to bring projects to life. While keeping true to our original mission, and maintaining our wide-ranging backlist titles, our most recent publishing focuses on bringing to the fore voices that reflect and appeal to our community at the university as well as the wider reading community of readers and writers in the UK and beyond.

@KU_press

This book was edited, designed, typeset and produced by students on the Kingston School of Art MA courses at Kingston University, London.

To find out more about our hands-on, professionally focused and flexible MA and BA programmes please visit:

www.kingston.ac.uk

https://kingstonpublishing.wordpress.com/

@kingstonunipublishing

@kingstonjoupubmedia

@kingston.school.of.art

www.ingramcontent.com/pod-product-compliance
Ingram Content Group UK Ltd.
Pitfield, Milton Keynes, MK11 3LW, UK
UKHW040639080525
5819UKWH00012B/145